Sandy Anderson

Wasteland Press
www.wastelandpress.net
Shelbyville, KY USA

The Last Hound
by Sandy Anderson

First Printing – November 2015
ISBN: 978-1-68111-075-2

Printed in the U.S.A.

0 1 2 3 4 5 6

To all my people:
Two legged,
Four legged,
and
Bright winged.

But to all who received him, who believed in his name, he gave power to become children of God.

JOHN 1:12

The Last
HOUND

1

SHE WAS HAPPY. SO VERY HAPPY. Now. The day had not looked too good at its beginning. A morning that had loomed grimly with too much to do and not much of it significant. Which of the insignificances would prevail? She would have had to make decisions about her time. Which choice would she later regret? Should she have launched into some other project, something more worthy of her attention and energy? Hindsight. Always providing at least a pinprick of self-recrimination. She could have done the *other* thing so much more effectively. So, already contemplating its ending, the new day had threatened to leave her dispirited and ineffective. She might have stood impotently in the middle of a room for minutes at a time, incapable of making a decision, doing nothing.

But here she was now, horseback. A second to decide to do it, a half hour to get it done. Everything else could be postponed until tomorrow. It would all look better then, and she would be cleansed and fortified by this outing.

Unconscionable, to leave so much work at home undone. And yet Angela felt justified.

The freedom, the horse under her, the hound running ahead. It had all been mandated by the phone call.

Mandated or not, it had not been easy. It was never easy anymore. It had cost her a lot of effort to back the truck under the trailer hitch. Backward and forward; a few inches off to the right, then to the left. Getting completely off course; then having to drive directly forward again, lining it up, and inching backwards, starting all over. And so on. She had had to make many leaps out of the truck to check her progress. Finally everything was aligned enough so she could give the trailer tongue a hearty shove with her foot. The cup on the hitch sank down upon the ball on the truck.

Andrew could have done it in a couple of minutes. But she had been hurrying so she could leave before he got back from town. A few minutes conversation with him, and she might have abandoned her resolve. A good and husbandly husband, he would have made her go back for her hat. He would have needed to know exactly where she was going. He would have reminded her that she might need gas. She was pretty sure she didn't.

The telephone call had demanded a vigorous response. A new energy had seized her, ignited her with new hope and satisfaction. Memories flared. Rekindled suddenly was the warmth of a friendship that had lain for some time unsavored. She had needed to move, to get out and do some reflecting.

She could have left Andrew a note, the way she used to do when he was gainfully employed. In those days he would have been happy to come home from work and find her scrawled message on the kitchen counter. Or at least he had said he didn't mind, as long as she got home safely and there was an outstanding dinner. But, she told herself, she could call him later on the cell, if she could reach him on it.

What an Andrew. Retirement had provided him with time and opportunity to become her supervisor. He was a kindly supervisor but, now, even though she had a fine new cell phone and a fine new truck and a fine old horse that was actually broke, Andrew had turned into a worrier. He worried about her and about the hound, too.

But she was too happy to take a chance on not going at all. Or even to delay the adventure for a minute. She knew she would be able to explain it all to Andrew later. Zelie, the hound, had not been invited on a horse outing for some time, and had been slightly mystified when Angela had caught the little horse and taken him away from his breakfast. This was not the way things were done. But the hound had stood watching, puzzled for only a moment, before she raced for the front gate ahead of them, demanding not to be left behind. She had leapt into the back of the truck, wild with joy at the unexpected adventure.

Hound in truck; horse in trailer. Angela had hoped all was in order with the various chains and switches; hoped she had a decent water supply; hoped she did not, in fact, need to stop for gas. Hoped she had not forgotten the bridle. But she had not stopped to check anything.

Once on the road, she could afford to watch for Andrew. She had wished, actually, that she would meet him on his way home from town. Town. Town was 'downtown,' the place where you picked up the mail if you didn't have a mailbox at your driveway. Where you could get a pretty good pizza or some Mexican food. You could buy your groceries and get a haircut. The library was downtown, and the Marshal's office, fire station and a few antique stores. Lots of things. Camp Verde had been Fort Verde, an army outpost in Apache land. It still retained a bit of an outpost attitude. She and Andrew loved it. Many people had retired here, but Andrew had commuted from here; they had raised their children here.

And here came Andrew back from town. He had recognized her truck and trailer from a distance, flashed his lights and slowed. They stopped beside each other, rolled down their windows and chatted briefly. He was happy to see she was happy and doing something that she liked. They could talk until another driver came up behind one of them. Small town benefits. What they were doing, heading in opposite directions, and now blocking other traffic, was known as a Camp Verde stop sign. Drivers sometimes simply *stopped* when they passed each other in the neighborhood roadways, to exchange pleasantries through their open windows. Other vehicles might pause behind them for a moment, too, the drivers usually waiting cheerfully for the chatters to move along.

But Zelie had been baying over the side of the truck, at Andrew's face peering from the window of his pickup, and also at a neighbor dog that was running and raging inside his own fence. They had cut the conversation short because of the ungodly racket, and driven on.

She had watched Andrew's truck receding in her rear view mirror. What an Andrew, she had thought again. He was so generous with his good wishes for her. He had left her with only one admonition. "Don't lose the puppy."

Puppy! A four-year-old, seventy pound goof ball. But Zelie was the only hound they had at the moment. Andrew had become quite attached to her.

She had not told him about the phone call. He would be very happy to hear about it when she got home. It would take a while to tell.

And then she had been truly on the road. She could reflect on that morning's telephone conversation.

Windwhisper! She had not heard from the girl in ages. "Whisper!" she had shouted into the phone.

"Well, yes," the girl had said serenely. "Only nobody calls me Whisper anymore. You were the only one who called me that. And the 'Windwhisper' thing was fake and a vanity, my child-of-the-New-Age name. My real name is Genevieve, of course, but most people call me Gen."

"You'll always be Whisper to me. Oh, I'm so glad to hear your voice!"

They had both been silent for a long moment, remembering each other's voices, each other's faces, the dismal, deadly time they had once endured together, and the deliverance they had shared. The understanding and affection that had grown between them in the following years was as solid as ever. Also unforgotten, but unspoken, remained that lingering sadness, the memory of the one whose unfulfilled, sorrowful life had played itself out in their company.

But they had not alluded much to that experience this morning. It was all in the past. They had discussed those events for several years before finally going their separate ways.

"Wait till you hear!" Genevieve Windwhisper had said. "Wait till you hear! It's been so long since I've talked with you, and I've moved more than once, and I'd lost your phone number I thought, and I got busy, and...Oh, how I've wanted to talk with you again lately. I miss you so much." She paused. "I have the best news, the very best news." Finally, she had said slyly, "Guess what?"

"What?"

"I have a baby!"

So that was it. The conversation had gone on for some time, with Whisper doing most of the talking. Angela had been amazed at the breathless happiness in the girl's voice. During the canyon misery they had experienced, she would not have dreamed Whisper could produce such a tone. This morning Angela had found it contagious. She had asked the appropriate questions and felt a profound contentment sweeping over her, a sense of fulfillment. Her own happiness had cried out for this readjustment of her day. This horseback time.

And here she was, readjusted, swinging along behind the dog. At the trailhead, it had not been as difficult as she'd thought to sling the saddle up onto the horse's back. She worked on his off side now, because of her increasingly useless left arm. But she had slung the saddle up fairly easily with her right arm and it had settled into place; the trailer hitch had served as an adequate mounting block; the horse had stood still for her. Once in the saddle, her woodenish knees had loosened up a little. Zelie had immediately forged ahead and the horse had stepped out, eager to be going somewhere again. It looked like it might turn out to be a pretty good day.

Angela decided to make a present of the whole day to God. The day so far had been a gift to her. She would give it back, an offering to the Holy Spirit. They were in the middle of the Easter Season, the incredible, joyful season of the Resurrection. At the end of it all, after the Ascension, would blossom the gift of Pentecost, the real beginning of the transcendent kingdom. The Holy Spirit, a wild wind blowing wherever He willed, would shower fire, light and truth upon the earth for everyone. Through the Church. Through creation itself. It was a time to look for beauty. She knew she would find it. For these few hours, it would be her only task. What a relief.

2

ANGELA WAS EAGER TO LEAVE THE MAIN ROAD, wanting to take no chances with Andrew's "puppy" and any passing pickups. Smart as she was, the dog was still an innocent; a careless bumbler, trusting everybody. They crossed over the road a couple of times, avoiding traveling on it as much as possible, until they came to a fence and a cattle guard. Here beside the cattle guard was an easy gate. They crossed the fence line and dropped down the hill to the left, into the sanctuary of the canyon. At last. The wide wash of Cherry Creek, stretched out before them.

At this lower elevation Cherry Creek was not a creek at all, but eased dryly along as sand on the level valley floor. Angela was not fooled by it. She had seen where it was born, high above her in the Black Hills. An intermittent streamlet, winding among homesteads and old orchards in the town of Cherry, it dropped dramatically into the Verde Valley, gaining power and momentum in rainy times as it roared downward between the mountain ridges. But in the rainless seasons, in this lower canyon, it became just Cherry Wash, a dry streambed surrounded by an unexpected variety of vegetation begotten by the seeds and cones which had been carried down from above. Ponderosa and piñon pines grew along its banks, mixed with cottonwood, black walnut and wild cherry trees. Farther along, it was populated with the stately streamside sycamores as well as many ancient, twisted hackberry trees and the usual desert vegetation.

As usual, whenever she was horseback, Angela felt aliveness and thoughtfulness consume her. Today she was simply a passenger. She didn't have to watch her footing or listen to her arthritic knees complaining, too much. She didn't get out of breath. This wash was like a highway. The horse went along on cruise control and automatic pilot. She gazed around.

It was good to be back. Back on a back. She had thought those days were behind her when her last horse had died. For some time there had been empty stalls at their place. An empty horse trailer. Dust on the saddles in the tack room. And indeed, she was not the horse person she had once been. But suddenly and unexpectedly there had appeared in her life this little bay Arab she was riding now, Little Big Man. Seeking retirement after a lifetime of endurance racing, he was just the sort of animal she needed if she were not to call it quits completely. 'An honest horse,' his former owner had described him. And he was. Well trained. Well used. A little tired, after hammering out mile after grueling mile in his long distance racing days, but still game. Very game. She was aging. He was aging. Angela figured the two of them would be around just long enough to see each other out. She and Little Big Man might have a few good years left in them. Together.

Little Big Man. Finally.The last horse.

And then there was Zelie. She crisscrossed the wash in front of them, disappearing into the brush, reemerging to check on the horse's progress. She was kind of a mama's dog for a big black and tan. An embarrassment of a hound, actually. Arizona hounds were usually lean hunting machines, kept on chains when not working, tails cropped, heads scarred. The lion hunters Angela knew had smiled at her indulgently over the years. Some of them, seeing her on foot hiking with a single hound, would shake their heads in disgust, calculating the waste of a good-looking hunting dog. Just the other day Angela had encountered a hound man on a dirt track with a couple of fancy redbones in the back of his pickup. He spied her hound. She spotted his. Zelie, she immediately assessed, was a much better looking dog than his. Of course, as they slowly passed each other in the middle of nowhere, they had stopped to chat through their rolled-down windows.

And of course he had asked the hound man's question: "You doing anything with her?" Meaning, do you track mountain lions? Hunt bears? Go coon hunting at night? Haul dudes with cameras on pack trips? Hound enthusiasts had extreme expectations. They demanded performance, and it was often arduous and deadly. You didn't ask people with German shepherds or spaniels what they did with their dogs, but hound people did demand stories about the late great 'Blue,' his distinctive voice, his ability to cold trail and his final lion hunt.

So here it came again, the perennial hound man query, "You do anything with her?" What could she say?

"No," she answered. "Not really. She's good company. That's all." They had laughed and he had driven on. But all her other hounds up until now had truly been seekers and rangers. Independent and fierce. Her own hounds, too, like the real Arizona hound packs, had been scarred and trail worn, snake bitten, caught in steel traps, sometimes mauled. But she had not lost one yet. To a dog, they had all died natural deaths and been buried at home. And now Andrew, in particular, did not want Zelie to be the exception. Andrew doted on Zelie.

Angela had not wanted another hound at all. Too old for that, too old. When bluetick Callie died, Angela's heart for hounds had withered. Callie had been her companion in that lonely and fearful canyon experience with Windwhisper. Whisper had loved the dog, too.

For some time Andrew had agreed. They were both too old to take on another hound. In fact, he had been the most adamant. "No more hounds!" But in his dotage Old Andrew had become suddenly more sentimental, if it were possible. In celebration of 49 years of marriage he had imported a pedigreed black and tan coonhound from Arkansas as a gift for her.

The puppy was an expensive hillbilly. Savagely focused on Angela's ankles, indifferent to affection, in fact grimly rejecting it, the puppy had seemed at first to live in a world of her own. Angela had worked with her for months to make her more dog-like. She had not wanted another wild thing, rampaging through the countryside, refusing to come when called. They had even invested in a trainer, whose stringent ways had been no match for the puppy's. Zelie had won round two. And round three. Reminding herself constantly, "Too old for this, too old," Angela had set about taming the dog herself. They had ended up babying her too much, and Angela had deliberately worked to make her attentive, dependent, and more or less obedient. So 'the puppy' had turned out to be a cream puff. She pretty much kept Angela in sight, whether she was on foot or horseback. Zelie the coonhound traveled blithely through life, enjoying other animals and children and, unlike any other dog Angela had ever owned, anticipating with surprising, boundless joy her visits to the vet.

And now here Zelie was, four years old and totally pristine. Not a scratch on her. She had her very own couch. Still, Angela felt that somewhere in the big black and tan there ran a vein of true houndness.

Zelie. The last hound.

Today Zelie had discovered a zone of small butterflies. She bayed and bounded after the yellow fluttering horde that swept across the sand. They reminded Angela of a flock of miniature birds, swerving and dipping in unison. When they finally rose and disappeared altogether, Zelie turned back, panting, and continued on with the horse. Life was good.

Angela wondered about water for the dog. She had brought Zelie's bowl in a saddle bag, but not a water bottle. She wished she had been more thoughtful. Too late now, but she did not intend to go far. And there was a dirt cattle tank ahead that she remembered from years past as offering at least a reliable muddy mouthful. They would check that.

Once again she settled into the reflection that the freedom of riding brought her. When she finished going over her conversation with Whisper, she thought back upon her meeting with Andrew along the road. Old Andrew, she sometimes called him fondly, to herself. The OA. She wondered if that was disrespectful. She and Whisper had laughed over this. After they had become friends, the younger woman admitted to her that when they first met, she had referred to Angela in her mind as the "OC." "Old Crone." Now *that* was disrespectful. But she and Whisper had grown to love and respect each other. And, as far as Andrew was concerned, he really was Old Andrew. He was the older of the two of them, by three years. He called himself an old geezer. "You young people," he would say about her troublesome ways. Yes, Angela thought, it was fair to think of him as the OA once in a while.

"Wait until *you're* seventy six," Andrew would tell her. "You'll find out what it's like to have nothing functioning the way it used to." And it was true that he was slightly more decrepit and less energetic than she, because of various illnesses he had endured. He was also becoming hard-of-hearing, or maybe it was hard of comprehending. Or both. Often she could not tell if he had misheard or only misinterpreted. If she were too casual or offhand in her remarks, or if she flung a word over her shoulder as she was leaving a room, she found herself having to repeat even the most trivial of statements. She was, slowly, learning to moderate her language, training herself to look Andrew in the eye and say only what needed to be said. And she, no spring chicken herself, was damaged goods too. She had suffered more from bodily mishaps and accidents than he had, and still suffered from them. He was the one who had to hunch over to find an object in a lower cabinet for her, and he often had to help her out of a chair. They agreed, however, that whatever wholeness they enjoyed separately became one workable, complete person when combined. In short, they needed each other.

Marriage. That was what it was all about. Real marriage. Angela worried about couples who now tended to drift into and out of "relationships" which, in spite of protestations of commitment, were not at all, in the end, committed. They were missing so much, she thought. She and the OA had been married for fifty something years. Towards the end, and that was the way she had to think about it now, their marriage had become strangely more complete and satisfying as their physical decline became more evident. She and Andrew were friends, but much more than friends. They had shared a lifetime together, shared children, enjoyed the company of the same animals. Prayed together. She wished she could find a way to explain it to herself and defend it to others in these times when marriage seemed to have fallen into such disfavor.

The new pope, Francis, or Pancho, as Angela secretly but respectfully called him, was zealous on behalf of marriage. But how many would avail themselves of his wisdom? Or the wisdom of his predecessors? His words about married love were profound and poetic. Angela scribbled some of them down from time to time. He had spoken of married love being bolstered by the love of Christ when "humanly speaking, it becomes lost, wounded or worn out." It had made her think of their own years. Years of swimming upstream together, facing obstacles, meeting adversity, were indeed wounding and wearing. She and Andrew, and countless other married couples, knew this well. The pope had not grown up in a vacuum. He called the path of marriage "a demanding journey, at times difficult, and at times turbulent," But, as Andrew and Angela were increasingly discovering, it was truly Christ's love and His upholding of the two of them that restored to them "the joy of journeying together." Angela liked this phrase of the pope's. It was this joy, the joy of journeying together; that was the kind of life Angela had wanted for Windwhisper.

Again she thought back upon the morning's conversation. She had waited for a long moment after Whisper's announcement of the baby. "And...?" she had finally prompted.

A hearty laugh from Whisper. "And..." she echoed. "I'm married. Of course I'm married. I'm really, really married. I'm so happy. I have honor. I'm a woman of honor. I thought you'd be glad to know."

"Yes," Angela had said simply. She was going to add something else, but Whisper had launched into a litany of praise for the baby. Angela found herself thunderstruck by the gifts, virtues, accomplishments and intelligence of someone two months old and in diapers. Not to mention the conversational and emerging literary skills.

"Where are you?" she had finally been able to get in.

"Shubert, Nebraska."

"What! Why?"

"Because I'm married." Whisper had then embarked on a recital of her husband's qualities, which seemed to be wonderful, but not quite as impressive as the baby's. Then she was back on the baby, a boy, apparently. No other baby in Shubert; no other baby in Nebraska; no other baby in the world. She finally paused.

"And…?" Angela asked again, sensing that Whisper was waiting for this.

"Oh, of course. Of course he's been baptized," Whisper assured her. "What do you think of that?"

Angela and Whisper had been silent for a moment. Then Whisper had asked hesitantly, "So, do you suppose we could say that something good has come from Mr. P.'s life? Something good even from his…wickedness?" In the face of Angela's silence, she had added shyly, "If it hadn't been for Mr. P. we wouldn't have met. And I would never have learned so much…from you. I wouldn't have my baby," she paused. "And my husband."

Mr. P., a desperate, tormented soul, certainly a tragic figure, had taught Whisper and Angela something, in that other canyon, something about fortitude, and hope, and trust. And faith. Angela had learned some things about herself.

"Something good," Angela had agreed, reflectively, into the phone. "Yes. Something good."

And that was it. She could hardly wait to tell it all to Andrew.

3

Now, suddenly, Angela felt herself enveloped by this present canyon, immersed in the hugeness of it. In its stillness. All at once her skin surprised her by becoming prickly.

She rode slowly for another moment. Then, thinking about Whisper and the marriage and the baby, still electric with joy and gratitude, she touched the horse into a lope. Or she would have liked to touch him into a lope. He lumbered into something resembling a rough hand gallop, his flat Arabian feet plowing the sand and throwing it up behind them.

"Sarah says you're supposed to be able to spring easily into a canter, and on the correct lead," she reminded him silently, working with hands and legs to adjust his gait.

"Yeah...and you're not Sarah," he retorted in his own silent and horsey way.

But he seemed to be enjoying himself, as she was. She doubted that after a year and a half he was still expecting her to ride like Sarah, who was younger and had been a much more experienced rider than herself. Every time Angela rode him she found herself grateful for the training that Sarah and her husband had put into him, for the miles he had covered. But now he was her horse. Hers and Andrew's. Andrew fed him. She rode him. They kept the name Little Big Man, because he was a big little horse, smart, with a big heart. They called him LB, for short. LB. Little Big. The last horse. Definitely the last horse.

They raced along, spraying sand. Zelie thundered behind them, forgetting, for a time, the butterflies.

But their dash was a short one. Around a bend they came upon a man striding up the wash ahead of them. He was marching along briskly, but at the sound of their sand crushing approach, he turned to look back briefly.

Angela slowed politely. She moved to the side of the broad corridor and gained on him at the walk. She made no attempt to call the over-friendly hound. It would be futile. She hoped the man had a sense of humor.

He appeared to. The dog, of course, had trotted over to him. He stood still, leaning slightly on an aluminum walking stick. When Zelie came close he casually held out a hand to her. Her tail was lashing in greeting, carrying her hips from side to side. He smiled and spoke to her. She was ecstatic.

Angela called a hello to the hiker, passed him, and stopped at a distance, waiting for the dog. She knew that a certain amount of time was necessary for these greetings.

The hiker was well equipped. A compact, reasonably sized backpack, something technical looking strapped to his leg, a tubular device that was probably a canteen, and the fancy hiking pole gave him a formidably professional appearance. Super trekker. It must have been his red sports car that Angela had seen parked in the rough lot at the trailhead. If she had ever found a vehicle there at all, it was usually a pickup with horse trailer, or a mud spattered Jeep. But, long and low slung, incongruous, this car had squatted close to the earth, and the thin film of dust that had settled upon its scarlet glossiness seemed almost a desecration. Yes, the man and the car were a pair. And not from around here.

Zelie completed the formal introductions and trotted off into the brush. Angela rode on.

The canyon was broad here. Floodwaters had swept and ground the sand along for thousands of years, cutting the channel ever deeper but leaving flatlands along the sides where thickets of mesquite and hackberry were almost impenetrable.

LB, expecting her to continue to be simply a passenger, was surprised when she suddenly reined him up a low bank and onto a grassy flat opening among the hackberry trees. The hackberries here were huge and old. Each tree was a decided individual, twisted, distorted, lovely. Their branches crossed over, under and around each other in wild abandon, seemingly at random. Their trunks were gnarly, rumpled and battered. Some leaned, arthritically. Some stood like soldiers, reaching skyward.

Angela had not been up on this flat in years, though she had crossed it many times on foot in the past. Where was the Malcolm J. Mackenzie tree? Things had changed.

She missed him suddenly. Dr. Malcolm J. Mackenzie. She missed the tree. She missed those early days of her youth when she had, whimsically and ironically, sometimes a little cruelly, been a namer. She still named things: animals, rocks, cars, and sometimes people. These days her names for things were less acerbic, somewhat kinder. Malcolm J. Mackenzie, the tree, had been named for her old college Shakespeare professor because it had had borne such an uncanny resemblance to him. Knobby and angular, the tree had sat perched upon itself as Dr. Mackenzie had perched upon his austere metal chair at the front of the classroom. The tree's roots were a platform of legs which twisted grotesquely around each other as his legs had done. Dear Dr. Mackenzie. His bony face had stretched in a perpetual grimace of sorrow, the same caricature of Greek tragedy that illustrated the covers of their Shakespearean dramas. But he wore a mask of comedy, too, when he practiced his wry wit, a broad, face-slicing beam that came as punctuation to whatever subtle, humorous point he had just made. His students, if perhaps they were caught off guard and had missed that point, were quick to catch the smile.

He must be dead now. When she had been nineteen he would probably have been in his sixties. She was now in her seventies. She had named the tree maybe forty years ago and had told Andrew about it. When was the last time she had hiked up this canyon and found the Malcolm J. Mackenzie tree?

No tree today. What did she expect? Maybe someone had cut it for firewood. She turned back across the flat and dropped down into the wash. The hound crossed the wash in front of them from one low bank to the other.

Angela looked back the way they had come. Here came the hiker again, seemingly unimpeded by the softness of the footing, marching along. He did not lean on the stick, but appeared to use it with a flourish, swinging it ahead of him from time to time before planting it again in the sand.

Embarrassed to be once again intruding on the man's solitude, Angela trotted LB ahead of him up the wash, calling Zelie to follow. The dog hesitated, thinking another greeting might be in order, but then came along.

Once around the next bend, Angela slowed, reflecting. She had the canyon to herself again. There was nothing to do here but look and listen and think.

How had they gotten old? They were older than Dr. Malcolm J. Mackenzie had been! Only this morning she and Andrew had indulged in another threadbare discussion about their future. They joked about the old folks home that might someday claim them.

"I wouldn't want to live in a terrarium," he had said.

"You mean an aquarium."

"No. A terrarium. Stretched out all skinny, flat and still upon a low twig like a gecko. With my eyes closed. Same color as the sand. And people looking in at me."

"I'd be there."

"You'd be a gecko too."

But they weren't quite ready for geckoland, she thought. Yet. She was still riding, once in a while. Andrew was still cutting their kindling and taking out the ashes in the winter and fixing up a little garden in the summer. And they had each other. They could laugh, and grumble together.

"Wake up," she had said cheerfully this morning. "It's a new day!"

"Just what I need."

Angela rode into another squadron of pale yellow, tumbling butterflies, flimsy, tiny, inconsequential except for their numbers. Zelie leapt at them, chasing them upward. They rose rapidly out of range and, finally, out of sight. Puzzled, Zelie snapped her head around to gaze over her shoulder, her tail curled over her back like a Pomeranian's. Ridiculous. When she did spot them again, she started barking treed, as if she were a real hound after a real lion. Pretty good bawl on a tree, Angela thought. A hound man would appreciate that voice.

The dog was already hot, and probably thirsty. But the dirt tank lay ahead on their right. And farther up the canyon, in times past, she had come upon trickles of water. Water coursed underground here, and sometimes it rose to the surface. Today they might get lucky. Way up the canyon, where the wash ended at the base of lava cliffs, long ago she had found a pool with a thin sheet of water sliding into it. She and other dogs had gone into that pool together many times. Years ago.

Years ago. Funny. It had been years since she had come to this place. Why had she chosen this route today? The Dr. Malcolm J. Mackenzie tree was gone. The intense Malcolm J. Mackenzie himself was no doubt gone. She and Old Andrew, themselves, were on "the slippery slope," as the OA called it. "One foot in the grave."

It couldn't be. Could it? The "one foot in the grave" part? But what were the odds? They had joked that the Second Coming might find them still alive and anticipating. They would be like the ancient prophet, Simeon, in the Gospel of Luke, and the equally ancient Anna. Those two had died happy after seeing at last in the Christ Child, the promised savior of the world. Maybe she and Andrew could be like Simeon and Anna. They would be around to greet Jesus on His return. But it had come to look as if *Someone*, she wouldn't name any names, was delaying His arrival.

As it turned out, time had passed rather swiftly, and here they were, she and Andrew, kind of...old. She herself didn't feel too changed, unless she happened to examine her elbows in the mirror. And, apart from the various accidents, the general and apparently unavoidable soreness and weaknesses of aging had arrived so gradually that it was only when sharply surprised by them that she noticed them much at all. They tried to make light of these things.

"I bet you never thought you'd be married to a rheumy-eyed old geezer," Andrew had said recently. "I've read about rheumy eyes in novels. Never thought I'd be wearing a couple of them." He dabbed at his eyes. "Rheum." Then he coughed dramatically. "Phlegm." He paused in thought. "Rheum and phlegm."

"And I'll bet you can't even *spell* rheumy," she had responded. She waited. Old Andrew, brilliant as he was, was still a notoriously bad speller.

He started out: "r-h-e," grew bolder, and finished with a flourish, "u-m-y."

She gave him the thumbs up. "How about phlegm?" She waited for him to launch out with an f., but he surprised her with the ph, and didn't forget the g.

"Good job," she said.

In smug triumph, he had given her a grin, then coughed and taken his handkerchief to his eyes. "Phlegm and rheum," he said again.

Old Andrew. How dear and funny he was. The last husband. The only husband.

4

SHE AND LB WERE APPROACHING THE TANK. A killdeer ran piping ahead of them on spindly legs. A killdeer was usually a sign of nearby water. A strange name for a bird, Angela thought. Some imaginative ornithologist had described its cry in her bird book as sounding like two words: "*keel deer, keel deer.*" It didn't sound like that to her! It was a noisy bird, however, always running and piping, running and piping. A member of the plover shore bird family, it still found its way to farmlands and even to deserts – wherever there was a little water. She loved these colorful, long legged sprinters.

Zelie climbed the sloping bank below the dirt dam and disappeared over the edge. Angela rode up after her.

The tank was dry. Mud at the bottom was crisscrossed with multitudes of tiny bird tracks and the hoof prints of javelinas. Zelie sniffed at the dampness and looked questioningly up at horse and rider.

"You're out of luck," Angela told her. She was still wondering which direction to take as she rode back down into the wash. With no water for the dog, maybe she should just turn around and head to the trailer.

Another killdeer sprang up from the sand near LB's feet. A female. Crippled and crying, she moved rapidly away from them, beating the earth ahead of her with one wing, dragging the other behind her.

Angela flung herself off the horse. She made a leap for Zelie and caught her collar before she could get to the bird. She had dropped the reins, but LB stood while she grappled with the lunging hound.

Angela heard a cry behind her. She turned. It was the hiker. He rushed toward them. She couldn't tell if he was trying to capture the killdeer to rescue her, or if he was attempting to help her with the horse and dog.

"Stop!" she shouted.

He obeyed.

"Please wait a minute," she said again more politely. "I'll show you something."

By this time she had LB's reins in hand again and Zelie's collar twisted tightly around her fingers. The hound sat, gazing after the bird, who continued to shriek and struggle in a pathetic circle some way ahead of them.

"Come on up here," she said to the man. "Go slowly, and watch the ground carefully." She peered at the ground, too. "A little more to the left," she said. "Slowly, slowly." She tried to focus on the place from which she had seen the female killdeer arise. The hiker was creeping toward her, glancing at her then looking at the sand. "Now," she said, directing him to one side with her hand.

"Stop!" she ordered again.

He stood still.

"Now, look straight down. Look all around right in front of you. Watch for a little depression in the sand."

"There it is," he said. "Oh. Oh my gosh."

"I want to look, too," she said. "I have to. I just can't not look. And then we need to get out of here. Poor Mama."

Angela, carefully leading the horse and hunching over the dog, went to stand beside the hiker. In the mottled sand, at the bottom of a shallow scraping, lay four speckled eggs. If she or the hiker had varied their line of travel by a foot, they would have crushed the mother's fragile treasure. How vulnerable they were. Almost indistinguishable from their surroundings. Yet in their camouflage lay their hope of safety from predators. In their camouflage and in their mother's bravery.

She studied the man as he bent over the nest. No, he was not a Camp Verde specimen. His khaki colored clothing was crisp and well pressed. From top to bottom, he looked as if he had stepped out of an L.L.Bean catalogue. He wore on his well-groomed hair an expensive sun screening hat, and on his feet leather hiking boots of good quality. Italian, maybe, Angela thought. She had owned a pair once. Another Andrew extravagance. Andrew was one for extravagances. He had bought her hounds, horse trailers, hiking boots over the years. She had loved her one pair of Italian hiking boots, literally, to pieces. When she had worn them to leather rags, she had refused to throw them away and had hung them in trees for birdhouses.

The man stood up and turned to her suddenly, catching her watching him. For only a moment he kept his unguarded expression of joy over the beauty of the sand nest, but immediately discretion ruled his features. Angela wondered at her first impression. He had swung the walking stick jauntily as he marched along, a happy young man out for a morning's walk. But now she sensed an unease about him. He smiled politely.

She smiled back. "Aren't they lovely? Isn't the mother wonderful? It was all a ruse. She was pretending to be injured to distract us and lead us away." He nodded and gave another, more generous smile. "OK," she said to him cheerfully. "We didn't see these eggs at all, did we?" She looked at the female. "Come on back, Mama. You saved your babies."

"You go ahead," she told him. "It's going to take me a while to get back on."

The man leaned over and took another long look at the eggs, then started off. He turned after a few feet and glanced back at the nest site, then at Angela's face. Giving a little conspiratorial wave, he crossed the wash and continued up it, deliberately giving the mother killdeer not so much as a glance.

Angela made the same maneuver. Ignoring the vigilant mother, she led her horse and dog over to the far edge of the wash. The killdeer, apparently restored to health, was by now running quite nimbly on her stilt legs back and forth across the wash in front of them with her wings folded neatly against her sides. Angela released Zelie, who had lost interest in the bird. A boulder made a good mounting block, but she waited until the hiker was well out of sight. It was embarrassing to have to struggle so to get on a horse. She had certainly not planned to get off, and she wouldn't do it again. She glanced back once. The mother bird was skimming over the ground on her way back to the nest.

Which way should she go? The presence of the two killdeers and their nest indicated that water must be somewhere nearby. She longed to find it. But if the water were there, it lay in the same direction the hiker had taken. She didn't want to come upon him again. She should just finish her ride and head home. But the dog was nowhere in sight. She turned upstream again, after the hiker, watching for Zelie.

She came upon the man again, passing him at a slow jog and giving him a wide berth. She turned in the saddle and waved back at him. A pilgrim, she suddenly thought of him. Yes, "The Pilgrim," hiking along so resolutely, as if he had a holy destination.

Zelie found them and they continued on.

One more bend, Angela told herself, as she had done so many times before. Just around one more bend in the wash, and if I don't find the water, I'll turn around and head for home. She watched the dog.

Zelie seemed to be doing OK. She was panting, and ready to rest from time to time. But she didn't seem to be in any distress. Angela settled into meditation again. What joy to simply think and not to have to talk. She congratulated the little horse occasionally on his manners, but that was different. Not talk at all. And every once in a while she spoke to a tree or a bird, but that was surely not conversation either.

She thought again of her strange, inordinate joy over the news of Whisper's marriage. Was it? Inordinate?

How had it come to be that the fact of an actual marriage could build such an emotion of gratitude in her? Was she totally out of step with the world? But Old Andrew was the same. She would hear him snorting over the obituaries in their thrice weekly newspaper.

"Another darlin' companion," he would mutter. "The old fool!"

Angela would know he was referring to the spate of hangers-on who seemed these days to be the survivors of the dead. "Partners" or "Life companions." When he discovered that someone was survived by a real wife who had shared his life for sixty-three years, she would hear him murmur something like, "Aww…" How predictable Andrew was these days. Full of love, really, for everyone. Maybe that was why he was so disturbed at the brevity of contemporary relationships and the insistence upon unseemly liaisons that were not marriages at all. "Open and notorious cohabitation! That's what they used to call it," he would say to the dog. "There used to be a law against it."

Strong words, Angela thought. Perhaps unkind in certain circumstances. But should human behavior really have changed this dramatically? She remembered when fathers would say, if they found couples spending too much time together, "What are your intentions toward my daughter?" Now people made up beds in the spare room for their daughters and their boyfriends. Couples bounced around from one intense relationship to another. The children coming from these unions were burdened with a lifetime of complex and confusing genealogy. And quite often with negligence and abuse. Young women struggled alone to raise babies and hold down jobs. Grandparents ended up raising little ones again. Or the babies were simply killed, taken from their mothers' bodies. Two or three short generations had served to accomplish all this. It seemed bewilderingly fast, and startling in its general acceptance. It appeared now to be inevitable. People shrugged. "What can *we* do about it?" Or, "Who am I to judge?" Others prided themselves on being loving and broadminded. Up to date. But the little children, Angela thought. The little children. It couldn't be right for *them.* Pope Francis, concerned for what he called "this damaging mentality of the temporary," was calling for a major new environmental focus, a radical approach toward protection of the social environment of children, for a "new human ecology." It would, certainly, be more human, she thought. She meditated for a moment on this idea of human ecology.

And as always, while the horse ambled, taking her away from ordinary concerns, her mind bolted. It raced away for a while after this idea of a human ecology. She savored it for some time, embellished it, made some adjustments, came to some conclusions. She was free to change her mind. Free to think. Think, or even better, she could silence her mind and wait. On the horse, away from the mess of necessity, bigger and finer ideas could visit. Fragments of poetry might come to her, visions of faces long departed, recollections of the loveliest of places.

5

SHE REMEMBERED, SUDDENLY, A SITUATION she had encountered in another canyon not long ago, an enigma of a canyon in the Vermillion Cliffs Wilderness area. Canyons. They seemed to be the locations for the most interesting events in her life. Mountain top epiphanies were not for her, apparently. She was no Moses or Elijah. No, for her it was the canyons. One canyon after another.

She had traveled that time without a dog, without a horse, without Old Andrew, returning to an area she had yearned to see again since childhood. As a child, a prisoner in cars pressing on to other destinations in northern Arizona, she had peered over highway bridges into deep gashes in the earth, drainages to the Grand Canyon. Those canyons! Over eons they had collected waters to pour into the Colorado River. What colossal landscapes even these side canyons had presented to her ever so briefly as she passed. She had promised herself that she would return some day to explore the starkness and the mystery of at least one of them.

And she had kept her promise. But in such a canyon, when she finally did return, she had felt a glimmer of fear as she trekked alone, in unfamiliar territory, a stranger in the vastness. A dog would have been a comfort, but also a worry. The walls of Cathedral Canyon, near Lee's Ferry, had loomed vertically, providing for a dog only a few brief ledges to invite exploration. Angela had been relieved that she would not have to see Zelie perched, trapped somewhere high above her reach, or plummeting over a cliff face in a dash after a chipmunk.

She had wandered along in the bottom of the canyon, taking her time, entranced by the transition in texture and color of the rock layers walling her in. Were these canyon walls actually growing above her? No. They couldn't be. It was the wash, seemingly level and smooth, that was dropping beneath her. She had felt she was magically descending through great unimaginable swaths of time, leaving the present age behind.

Nothing stirred. No one knew where she was. It was what she had imagined she was in need of. Solitude. A car at the trailhead had indicated other hikers, but so far there had been no sign of another human.

Silence. Down through a layer of the Chinle Formation, then another formation. And another. Some of the rock strata were so thin she could practically feel them washing and sloshing along as the shallow platforms they had once been, at the bottom of vast prehistoric seas. Other layers were twelve or fifteen feet thick, where ancient debris had settled. Every level displayed distinct coloration. Teal, grey, pink, lavender. Downward she traveled as the walls rose around her. The decline was gradual, but always dropping toward the Colorado River. The big river ahead of her was also dropping, she knew, still cutting its own way through rock layers as if trying to penetrate to inner Earth. She had half imagined she would actually reach the Colorado that day, something she had always longed to do. The canyon floor became a highway carrying her inexorably toward a meeting with that long and significant river that collected the waters of most of the rivers and streams in Arizona, defined the borders of states and finally poured itself out into a different nation. The Colorado. The color of red, as it used to be before the dams. Her own river, winding close to her pastures back at home was the color of green. The Verde. The Verde River, too, by way of its sister rivers, finally found its way to the Colorado as it made its way on to the Gulf of California in Mexico. She delighted in contemplating the pathways followed by streams and rivers. How connected everything was.

But there would have been no escape for her from this Cathedral Canyon. A flashflood would have had its way with her. She had examined the sky. It was clear. No sign of rain where she walked, but that was no real reassurance. And she was very much alone.

Then a torrent of birdsong had cascaded into her solitude from the rim of the canyon. A canyon wren's joy. She knew who the little bird was and what he would look like. Such a magnificent noise from such a tiny beak. The purity of the notes falling around her, descending from the heights as bubbles rippling downward on the musical scale, brimming with light and happiness, brought Angela to a halt. Over and over the bird called. Once she caught a glimpse of the fervent creature flitting high above her among the rocks at the very top of the cliff.

She had stood enraptured, remembering the poet Shelley and his 'Skylark.'

"Hail to thee, blithe Spirit! bird thou never wert, that from Heaven or near it, pourest thy full heart in profuse strains of unpremeditated art."

This bird, her bird, pouring forth its full heart, had been just a tiny canyon wren. But it was indeed a blithe spirit.

And so had Angela been, suddenly. Blithe. The silence, the stillness, when it came again, was a commanding presence. Yet it had carried the memory of the birdsong. She had walked on in joy within it.

But in a short while the canyon had lent her a challenge. It dropped away beneath her feet, the broad pathway of sand resuming at the bottom of a jumble of wedged boulders. It was no steeper than many a descent she had made. She had looked down, considering. It was only a distance of some forty feet, but still at a sharp enough angle to demand some caution from her on the way down, and a great deal of concerted effort on her way back up. Perhaps there were other drop-offs, even more menacing, between the river and her.

Should she insist on going on? She had dawdled at the edge of the boulder tumble until she spied a couple of hikers moving up the wash toward her. A man and a woman, carrying packs. She had stepped aside to permit them to ascend the rough ramp unobserved. She could ask them about their experience of the river route when they reached the top. She had watched the beginning of their climb. The man's pack was strangely large and awkward. Skilled climbers, they had picked their way rapidly upward, among and over the boulders.

Angela had moved away, into some shade, to wait for them.

Then suddenly a canyon wren's song had come again. A clear yodel, this time, full of happiness, but not quite right for a bird. Angela had hurried back to the edge of the drop-off to look down. The man's pack was moving independently, as if struggling to detach itself from his body. Angela gazed in amazement. From the top of the pack, under a kind of canopy, something surged outward. A pair of chubby arms. A rounded profile thrusting forward. The wren song came burbling out of this little face. The fingers, curling, stretching, grasping, reaching downward, seemed to strain for the steep crush of boulders below, as if to seize them for an everlasting moment. The baby's voice was full of joy, unafraid, challenging. The pack shifted from side to side on the man's shoulders as it hung over the precarious route, traveling upward. The baby sang, in its own private language. A girl baby, Angela decided. She did not know why. The couple climbed bravely.

Angela had been filled with love for the little family.

Reluctant to intrude, she had let them pass along with only a wave. Curious, she thought. After sharing that strenuous hike and climb, they seemed to have nothing to say to each other. They marched along grimly, but she heard the baby singing until they were well out of sight. She waited for a minute and then she turned and retraced her route to the Jeep. She knew she would never follow Cathedral Wash to the big river. She was too old. It was all right.

At the trailhead another car had pulled in beside Angela's and the one belonging to the young couple. A group of hikers were disembarking from it, adjusting packs, tightening boot laces.

Baby Wren was still imprisoned inside her aluminum and canvas conveyance. She was propped upright against the back bumper of her parents' car, as if she were another piece of equipment among their assortment of gear. The young wife was organizing, stowing things away in the trunk. The husband was nowhere in sight. After a time, with everything packed away except the baby in her carrier, the woman had approached the departing hikers.

"My boyfriend came up the trail ahead of me," she said. "Have you seen him?"

'My boyfriend.' Angela still recalled the acute, unreasonable disappointment that had consumed her at those words. A man, a woman and a child. They were not really a family after all.

My boyfriend. Was that the best that could be said about the baby's father? Was he even the father? The couple perhaps had no claim upon each other, except for the lasting one that the baby might exert upon her mother.

For Angela, the knowledge had landed like a blow. They had been so beautiful in the canyon. The beauty had been stolen from her.

While the mother chatted with the other hikers, Angela had wandered over to look down upon the baby. As she approached, whatever of the little one's anatomy was not swaddled grew wildly animated. Her arms reached and swung; her female face had rippled in a wide, toothless grin.

"Hey, little canyon wren," Angela said to her. "Hey, little one."

As she spoke, the young man had come to the parking lot from a different direction, scowling at a camera he held, offering no greeting to the young woman or the baby.

"Where were you?" the woman demanded. He had shrugged exaggeratedly. He owed her no explanation. He owed her nothing.

Sick at heart, Angela had said a prayer over the baby and driven away. She still said a prayer for Baby Canyon Wren from time to time.

But this morning she had discovered that somehow, against the world's prevailing semi-logic, she had managed to convey to her very funny young friend, Windwhisper, the need for it. Marriage. A life sustaining nourishment of soul and body of man and woman, given by, and for, each other.

Angela had talked about these things with Whisper some years before, when their ordeal in the other canyon had been the genesis of their friendship. She and Whisper had survived together. They valued each other. They had lost track of each other. Now they had found one another again. It even appeared that Whisper had, indeed, listened to her.

Whisper had a baby. Whisper was married! The baby was baptized. Old Andrew would be grateful for all this news. Marriage was interesting. Old people who had been married for a long time were interesting. Babies who came along in due course were interesting. Other arrangements, other "relationships," temporary and soulless, were not interesting. They were, in a word, boring. Futile, eventually.

"Aww…" Andrew would say when a car would pass them on the highway proclaiming 'Just Married!' in a rear window.

It wasn't pinch-faced disapproval toward the young and the passionate that she and Andrew felt. They had been young and passionate themselves. But they had always recognized a higher purpose for their union, and it had settled in upon them more deeply as the years passed. She wanted the same thing for everyone, something if not necessarily sacramental, at least lasting, transcendent. For Andrew and her it had been a sacrament. Painful. Glorious. Transformative. Eminently satisfying. Eternal.

Marriage. It came from God.

6

NOW HERE SHE WAS, IN YET ANOTHER CANYON, closer to home. Today's canyon. She needed to pay a little attention to it. There was no water here in Cherry Wash except for an occasional dampness in the sand, at which the hound sniffed. Not enough to make a trickle. Angela thought of the killdeers, who had made their hopeful, modest nursery near the dirt tank, which had failed them. She said a prayer for the little killdeer family and glanced upward. No sign of rain clouds.

She needed to turn back. Perhaps around the next bend. The horse was of course not yet tired at all, but the hound was mostly trotting behind them now, her tongue out. Angela knew, however, that Zelie would still be interested in a chase, should something interesting turn up.

The pool that she remembered at the far end of this long canyon began to beckon. It had once been her own holy destination. 'Springs of life giving water,' descending from the heights. The water had been a balm, for her and her other dogs, those years ago, when she had been able to hike the distance. On a horse, today, it would be easy, but there was this puppy to consider.

Zelie darted off after another set of butterflies, baying.

Angela made the decision to try for the waterfall and the pool. It would be something to tell Andrew if she could see that place once again. It occurred to her that it would probably be the last time. So many things they did now they realized were probably for the last time.

For all their joking, they shared a trace of unacknowledged fear. Things went wrong with their bodies. Friends died. Animals died. The old apple tree toppled over. Their own death was finally, truly, staring them in the face.

Yet here she was, riding again, a few weeks into the Easter season. A Resurrection mentality was what was called for. Reading the old pope's book on the life of Christ, she had been stunned to discover that there was a much better way to define the resurrection event. Christ's rising from death was a great deal more than the "resuscitation of a corpse," Pope Benedict XVI had said. Jesus had entered into and introduced an entirely new dimension. He was alive! Even more alive than He had been on earth. She was alive, too, and much more than simply alive, because of what He had done. True, for her the next step of the process would be an unfamiliar, unparalleled and probably rigorous, adventure. Death. And then, voila! An entirely new Angela. A new, and possibly young, Old Andrew. And even now, on this earth, they could already be somewhat newer, if they wanted to.

She gave LB a signal, and he sprang forward. Zelie charged in their wake, bellowing with joy.

When she slowed again, she realized the canyon was closing in on them and they were nearing the end of the avenue of sand. Ahead of them the rugged hills converged, becoming ridges and ledges and gorges for the passage of Cherry Creek from the heights. The dog was showing unquestionable signs of being tired and thirsty. Angela stopped for a minute so Zelie could flop down beside them. The horse and the dog had become a pair in the short time LB had lived with them. Even their colors were complementary: copper red with black markings for the horse, black with copper gold points for the hound. They made a handsome couple. Today they shared the scanty shade companionably. LB hiked up a hind leg and dropped a hip to rest. Angela was canted over onto one side by the horse's crooked stance. She took a foot out of a stirrup and sat over on the other side to compensate, but did not dismount. Too much trouble to get back up. Zelie scratched a hole in the sand and stretched herself out in it. Peace.

They remained resting for a while, before starting out again. Now, nearing the end of the open wash, she discovered it had been battered into a boulder choked pit by descending floodwaters. They were stopped by the caving off of a steep bank into a large depression. The pool of water at the base of the first real cliff would lie ahead. It was just out of sight, but Angela could tell by the vegetation that some water could still be found there. Where the canyon walls closed in and the waterfall slid down over the rock face into the little pool, a brighter set of trees was growing, taking their refreshment from the damp sand that was all that remained of the creek itself. From where she sat on the horse, halted by the open cavern, she could see only the tops of the greener trees. She thought she could almost smell the water. It was tantalizing, but the way seemed to be closed to the horse. The hound lifted her nose.

"Go on," she told Zelie. "Go get a drink. It's right up ahead."

But the hound refused to leave them. Angela looked to the hillsides for a way around. Too steep, too rugged and brushy. She looked down again. Perhaps if they climbed down into the trough they could find a way up and out at the other end. Ahead of them the water beckoned. LB hesitated at the brink and she held him back a moment. She was not eager to drop into that ominous looking pit. Was she, now that she was old, losing what was left of her nerve?

"Go on, now," she said again to the dog, firmly. "You can do it, silly. You don't need me. Go get a drink."

Again Zelie lifted her head and sniffed at the breeze. Angela knew she could smell the water. She whined and looked up at the horse.

"All right," Angela told her. She put LB to the descent and they slid to the bottom in a cloud of dust. What a horse. Again she was grateful for the years and miles he had spent with Sarah. Now he was a good old horse for an old woman. A good Arab. Her horse now. The last horse. Had to be.

The debris from past floods made a formidable barrier. Uprooted tree trunks mixed with new growth that was already beginning to claim the area. They picked their way among boulders and over cross-hatched logs and twisted brush. Angela was amazed at the transformation in the wash's landscape. No doubt it had taken many floods to excavate the streambed to this depth at this particular location. Many floods over many years. Had it really been so long since she had come here? She looked for a break in an impenetrable log-jam before them. Would it be possible to lead the horse around? Dismounting, she brought LB behind her around the crush of tree trunks and branches and up along the bottom of the sloping bank that now rose beside and above them. The sand sifted downward beneath them as they scrambled along lopsidedly at the bank's lower edge. LB's off side legs were uphill, his near legs downhill. The little bay trod cautiously, careful not to crowd her or step on her feet. The hound followed, not so carefully, bumping up against the horse's hocks from time to time.

They cleared the last wedge of driftwood and found themselves in a curving impasse, blocked by huge boulders at the base of a runoff. Here was where the water had once pounded down to dig this channel. It had formed its own cliff. There was no way the horse could go on.

Angela pondered. She could go ahead on foot, taking Zelie, doing a little climbing, but she hesitated at tying LB by the reins and leaving him. If he did break away and head for home, she would have a long, long way to walk.

"It's right *there*!" she said to the dog. "Water! Get on up there. *Go* now!"

But Zelie smiled happily at her, tongue lolling, saliva dripping, and whined again, waiting for Angela to come along.

"You're worthless!" She shook her head in disgust. Any of her other hounds would have found a way to the water, wallowed around in it, lapped up copious amounts and come back to her ready to follow her or to seize upon another hunting opportunity. But there it was. This last hound was what she had wound up with. In a way she was glad that Zelie wanted to remain so close. She was too old for worrying about and searching for lost dogs. This last hound was what she herself had made her. A wimp.

She gave up. The water had been so close. "OK," she said in resignation, ruffling one of the long ears. "But you're going to regret this." She looked back over the way they had come. Daunting. She was thirsty, too.

She looked up at the bank beside them. There seemed to be a little space at the top of the slope before the brush closed in on it. Maybe a ribbon of cow path. "Let's try climbing up here," she said to the two of them. She took a good hold on LB's reins and he came up the crumbling bank behind her. She had to move out of his way a few times as he lunged, but he was careful not to climb over the top of her or to surge on ahead. She herself slipped backward a few times and had to grab a stirrup for support. She didn't even look for the dog. And suddenly they were on more level ground on the narrow trail, turned around and headed for home.

It was rough going for a while. She had to remain on foot and thread her way through the brush which closed in on them rapidly. She was not able to spare the horse, but only to trust him. Having to watch her own footing, she could not afford to look back at him and encourage him along. But he followed willingly. At one point she forced herself through a tangle of desert willows, and she felt him begin to hesitate. She glanced back. A branch had wedged itself under the pommel of her saddle and was holding him there. She tried to back him for release, but the branch went with him. She tried to shift it herself, but it clung stubbornly. There was nothing else to do. She asked him to come forward again and he strained against the branch as it bowed and, finally, snapped. She pulled the leafy remainder of it out from under her saddle, trying not to look at the new gouge it had left in the leather. Andrew would notice that first thing. Why hadn't she thought to simply take the saddle off? She must be getting tired. Or old.

They went on. LB ducked when she ducked, paused when she paused, climbed over when she climbed over.

At last they came back to the wide expanse of wash. It was a relief to find themselves surrounded again by open space. It seemed as if they had escaped something, but there were still some miles to go toward the trailer and home, and Angela was not yet back in the saddle.

It was true. She was suddenly very tired. She looked for the closest large boulder and led the horse to stand beside it. She climbed up onto the rock. It wasn't easy. It was at a good height and would put the stirrup within reach, but the rock was rounded and tried to teeter with her. She steadied herself. LB was a little far forward. She leaned over and eased him back a step with the reins. But now he was a bit farther out. She was well into this project. She didn't want to dismount the rock to mount the horse. She could have done this easily in her youth. Or even a couple of years ago. The OA used to be able to fling himself on a horse bareback. But here was the stirrup, certainly within reach. She stuck her left leg out tentatively and caught it with her toe. The boulder turned. She winced as she gripped the pommel with her left hand and heaved herself forward. As she lunged for the saddle, she needed to swivel her leg, and she did. But LB shifted at the same time, calling for more swivel than she had planned. She flopped over onto his off side, with her left leg and the stirrup following over his rump. For a minute she dangled there, clutching his mane. Her right leg hung close to the ground, almost touching, but it was not touching. Her face was against the horse's shoulder. She could smell the sweet, wholesome horsiness of him. She would not mind dying with that smell in her nostrils. But she couldn't just hang here. She had remembered to tighten the cinch earlier, one bit of good sense, at least. The saddle had not come over with her.

LB stood, good horse that he was. He dropped his head a little and she leveraged herself up onto his back, using her right elbow across his neck.

She sat there in the saddle, sobered by the helplessness and fear she had felt. Had she prayed? She couldn't remember. She hoped so. Her left knee throbbed.

Everything was in place, but what if it hadn't been? What if she had completed her acrobatic maneuver and he had run, carrying her upside down along the canyon at top speed? She was suddenly and excruciatingly aware of her frailty and her age. She was old, certainly too old to continue to be so imprudent. Newspaper articles chided the lost hikers or riders who went without companions into the wilderness, who neglected to take water, who, heaven forbid, rode helmetless. For herself, she had always trusted in Divine Providence. But now, for a long moment, she was embarrassed and contrite. She wasn't invincible, after all. What if she had been killed? What about Andrew? What would he do without her? She resolved to be more careful. She also resolved not to tell him about her near wreck. At least for a while.

They set off slowly. Angela was for a time a bit trembly. LB did not hurry. Zelie trotted along at their heels. They stopped often in a patch of shade for her. The fresh April morning had turned into a hot afternoon. The butterflies must have become dispirited and retired for a siesta. Angela was grateful to see no sign of them. Zelie didn't need another frantic chase. What kind of butterflies were they? Why did they go about in daffodil-colored gangs at this time of year? What was their next project? She only seemed to notice them in the early spring. Angela had tried once to find them in one of her field guides, but she was still mystified. There were so many things that she longed to know. Was all this knowledge to be saved for another lifetime? No. Another dimension. Eternity. Something else to look forward to. She hoped it wouldn't be too soon.

The aloneness, now that she was safe, began to feel good again. The horse, moving homeward, began to step along a little faster. The hound, her black body absorbing heat, her dripping tongue dispelling it, was satisfied to remain with them in the wash.

They paused again in the dense shade cast by a juniper. The sand here was cool, and Zelie stretched out on her side close to the horse's feet, trusting him. Angela raised herself in the stirrups to stretch. Her left knee was sore, and she wouldn't be able to do much at all with her left arm for a few days, but otherwise she seemed to be in pretty decent shape. It would be good to get home. Maye Old Andrew was already coming up with an exotic dinner. Zelie scrambled around in the sand, flopped over and cooled her other side. The silence of the canyon was a balm to Angela. Even her thoughts had stilled. She was glad to have the dog resting. The three of them were so quiet that a Steller's jay floated into the branches near them. It shook itself, reached around, and began to draw a brilliant blue tail feather through its beak. When it looked up and discovered someone already occupying its territory, it made a harsh comment and flew off in disgust.

7

ZELIE PICKED UP HER HEAD AND GAZED AROUND.

"Just stay with us," Angela told her.

But something had caught the hound's attention. She sprang to her feet and stood, puzzled. Angela could see nothing.

Then Zelie burst out into the sunshine again, pouncing with her front feet, first in one direction, then another, peering at the ground. Angela could see nothing to cause such excitement. She started the horse down the wash again, hoping Zelie would follow, but the dog swept around them, focused intently on the sand, way too energetic, Angela felt, for this heat. Suddenly Angela saw what she was after. Shadows dancing across the sand. She looked up. There were the butterflies, flying higher, too far overhead for the dog to see. But their shadows were very distinct. The sun was high enough and the seemingly fragile bodies substantial enough that the shadows became darting black targets on the bright whiteness of the gravel. Zelie raced feverishly after the phantoms, head down, baying. Angela had to laugh. But she called to her to come away. The dog must be almost at the point of exhaustion. She called again. Zelie ignored her. She raced and doubled and spun, obsessed. The butterfly silhouettes crossed the wash and were blacked out for a moment by the shade among the trees there. Angela hoped that was the end of it, but then the real butterflies veered and their shadows came tumbling back, luring the dog down the wash ahead of them.

Angela called her again. Zelie paid no attention. Exasperated, she finally shouted, "Get over here, you damn fool!"

There was a movement upon the opposite bank. It was the Pilgrim. He had been resting on a sycamore root in the shade. Now he rose obediently and started toward her. Angela was overwhelmed by a ghastly embarrassment.

She waited until he was closer, so she would not have to raise her voice again.

"Oh," she said, laughing. "I'm so sorry. I wasn't talking to you. I'm so sorry. My dog is being ridiculous and I wanted to get her attention. I didn't know you were there."

"That's all right. In truth, I think I *am* a damn fool. What is she chasing?"

"She's a hound," Angela laughed. "Not a coonhound or a lion hound, but a butterfly hound. At home she chases ravens."

The dog trotted up to them, her tongue hanging, tail at half-mast.

Angela surveyed the Pilgrim's equipment. "I didn't bring water," she said. "Could I borrow just a little of yours?"

He hesitated for a moment, then unsnapped the aluminum canister from his belt. She was starting to dismount when he stepped forward and handed it up toward her. He hesitated again and drew the bottle back slightly. He looked up into her eyes. There was a question in his own eyes. And a taut defiance playing at the corners of his lips.

"I'm gay," he said.

Angela sat back in the saddle. She did not reach out to take the bottle, but turned away from him to dismount, lifting her right leg slowly over LB's back. She stood for a moment in the left stirrup, getting ready, and then, both feet free, she let herself slide carefully down the horse's side, sparing her left arm and the aching knee as much as possible. An awkward dismount. It always was, these days. This time she took even longer. When she was firmly on the ground, still she did not turn to face him.

Some response was expected of her. What? Andrew had been a college professor. She and Andrew had known people in that oh, so progressive atmosphere who were "coming out" long before it became fashionable. Now it was all the rage. Still…it was not something she had expected today. Not something she felt she would ever have to deal with. And why had he assaulted her with this information? She remained at the horse's side, fumbling a bit with the saddle pouch. Here she was in the middle of a wilderness, riding along in peaceful solitude, and all of a sudden the day had turned upside down. The eternity of those ponderous seconds was apparently not as long as she had thought, however. When she finally turned to the man with Zelie's collapsible bowl, he was still holding the water bottle out to her.

"It's for the dog," she said crisply. She took the bottle from him, shook the bowl open, and poured in a very spare amount, careful not to spill any.

They both leaned toward the hound, watching her sloppily consume the water. Zelie looked up at Angela with a wag, and Angela gave the man a questioning glance. He nodded, and she poured in another small amount.

"That will do for her," she said. "I have water back at my truck." She handed him the bottle. "Thank you."

He was silent. That wasn't fair, Angela thought. It was his turn to say something. Some word of explanation was necessary. 'I'm gay.' His voice had held a ring of conviction, yet there had been a hint of doubt behind the words, as if he were proving something to himself or trying something out. Still, the easy, crystal familiarity of the day had been shattered. Why had he made that announcement? Was it because of the intimacy and pleasure they had shared at the discovery of the killdeer nest? She had sensed a hesitancy in him then, but she herself had been open and certainly she had not been threatening. What was she supposed to do now? He said nothing, waiting.

"Well," she began slowly. It was the longest well she had ever said, and she had dragged out quite a few of them over the years, especially with her children. She sighed. Suddenly she felt motherly toward him. She *was* old enough to be his mother, maybe his grandmother. He was much younger than her children, in his thirties, probably.

She looked kindly at him, she hoped, but she looked directly into his eyes, and his eyes held steady.

She glanced around as if she might find either someone to hold her back or someone to encourage her. Nothing but wilderness. Without boundaries, without walls. No disapproval and no guidance. No embarrassed observers. Nothing to restrain her. His soul was pulsing in front of her. He had offered it to her. She held it in her hands. She had seldom felt so vulnerable, not so much for the fact that if he felt like it, he could strike her with his walking stick, but that her words, if they came, must come unimpeded by social considerations. He had invited them.

It was as if the two of them were floating in a remote galaxy beyond earth's gravity.

But after all, she had no power over him. The situation seemed to call for a kind of irresponsibility. No one was watching. The dog had disappeared. The horse was uninterested.

It had been a long time since she had said the "Well…"

"Well," she said again. "You're not. And you're not."

"Not?"

"What you said."

He laughed and shrugged. "You know better than I do, I guess. You said it twice. I'm not and I'm not."

"I know some things," she answered, more bravely than she felt.

"Tell me," he said.

What was this? He must have had this conversation before, either with himself or with others. He had obviously resolved some things for himself in this regard. Or maybe he was questioning. Maybe he really didn't know what to make of himself. But what did he expect to accomplish by accosting a gnomish old woman on a horse in a canyon? Maybe a fresh point of view? She certainly did not want this dialogue.

"Well," she said again, slowly. Her favorite expression, apparently. But she went on. She seemed to be in this up to her neck. "You used a word. A word to describe yourself."

He nodded.

"You're not that," she went on. She knew she was right about this. She had looked into his eyes and seen the shadows like bruises around them and, deep within, the melancholy. Sorrow of long standing. "You're certainly not that. Not…gay." She hesitated for a moment. She looked down and he looked down, briefly. "You're sad."

"And are you simply taking exception to a *word*?" he asked.

Angela felt some long-suppressed grievance rising within her. Words *were* important. She felt a need, suddenly, to defend something precious. The general populace was trying too hard, way too hard, to take the heart out of the English language. The crispness had receded from it, the clarity, the force. No one died anymore, not even dogs. They passed. People used to grow corn. Now they grew their businesses. According to public announcements about crime, now every male was a "gentleman." Police reports quoted in the news tactfully declared that "the gentleman then exited the vehicle," when, in reality, a ruffian had leapt from a police car spitting, kicking and swearing. Only recently she had spoken to a friend about writing a fairy story for her grandchildren, and the woman had warned her, "Don't call it a *fairy* story. You can't say that word anymore."

The word "gay," of course, had been co-opted at first by a few pathetically trapped in the situation, and now by legions of activists agitating for social change.

Sorting old photographs recently, she had come upon a picture that her mother had long ago mailed to her aunt. The aunt had died and some of her personal effects had gotten back to Angela. There in the photograph was the young, grinning Angela, happily and unselfconsciously peering through a pair of new glasses. On the back her mother had penned: "Our Angela is a gay little girl." Angela's heart had turned mushy with nostalgia for a moment at her mother's description, but it had immediately occurred to her that even her mother would have been reluctant to use that word today.

Why should the world be robbed of a venerable and perfectly useful word? She sought, and found, the Pilgrim's eyes again. "Gay," she said forcefully, "means happy."

"It has another meaning which I am sure you are well aware of. Anyway, I *am* happy. Do you have any reason to believe I am not? What makes you think I'm not happy?"

"Because I can see you're not. And because you call yourself that. You're trying to say something about yourself that isn't true. That's why I said you're not and you're not. You're not happy." She paused for a moment, thinking. Was this even her business? But again she thought of how he had approached her. "And, here's the deal: the other thing that you say, about what you are, is not *who* you are."

"Who am I, then?"

"*I* don't know. You're a nice man hiking up a canyon. You haven't told me your name." She waited. When he didn't answer, she announced, "My name is Angela." She looked around for a place to remount. The situation looked bleak. She didn't want to struggle and claw her way up into the saddle in his presence. The bank was nearby, but on the wrong side of the horse.

"I need to turn him," she said. "Could you move out of the way? Please?" He moved obediently and she turned the horse and stepped up onto the low bank. It was easy to reach the stirrup from there. Once she was in the saddle, she felt less vulnerable. She gathered LB with the reins, preparing to turn him again and ride on down the wash, but the young man stepped closer.

"So you're saying that I'm not what I told you I was. What do you know about this sort of thing?"

"Well," Again! Her favorite word. Had she been stalling for time? So she rushed on, recklessly, seizing upon the first thing that popped into her mind. "Surely you have other interests."

"What!" he said incredulously.

"You seem to be consumed by this idea you have of yourself. Isn't there something else? You collect stamps? You're an astronaut. You're a gourmet cook." She paused and made a wry smile. "You're a Republican."

He laughed.

"You see what I mean," she went on. "You're a man. You're educated. You have a family somewhere. You've done lots of interesting things in your life. You read books. You appreciate nature." She let go of the reins and began to flap her arms around expansively. LB started to move off. She corrected him without interrupting her monologue. "You've been scared. You've been happy. You've eaten ice cream. Have you discovered enchiladas?" The Pilgrim was staring at her. She was winding down. Finally. The horse sighed. "You love dogs."

There seemed to be nothing to add to her litany. Only her theme remained.

She ventured back into his silence. "So maybe you've done something you're not proud of. Something unnatural. Or maybe you only think you *might* want to do something…ugly. Maybe something was done *to* you, when you were little. That doesn't *define* you." She waited for a moment, looking into the distance over his head. "None of this is *who* you are."

"Who I am," he echoed meditatively. "And who are *you*? Aside from being a rustic I ran across in a canyon, I mean."

"I'm a woman who sleeps with her husband," she snapped at him. "But I certainly don't define myself by that. In fact, polite people don't talk about these things!

He was silenced again for a moment. But he was persistent. "You still haven't told me who you are."

8

A RUSTIC! ANGELA WAS STILL FEELING THE STING of resentful humiliation. But what was she doing? She was amazed at her childish urge to defend herself. Should she tell him she had poured tea for the Poet Laureate of Great Britain? She had. In London. England. In a very stylish dress. It was a big event in her life, but it was certainly not part of who she was, and to speak of it would be continuing the argumentative and hubristic turn the conversation seemed to have taken. The whole encounter with him was already ludicrous. Yet she was sorely tempted to prove something to him. So what? She knew how to pour tea. It was something she had once done as a college student, an honorary sort of thing, shamefully artificial. A visiting professor from England had arranged the trip and the ceremony for her and for several others among his favorite students. Why had she thought of it? And what would it matter to this man, an absolute stranger standing in the middle of Cherry Wash? She had gone far enough. She decided against the tea pouring. She would remain rustic. Old Andrew was not going to believe this one!

The Pilgrim was waiting to hear from her. Was she about to say "Well" again?

"Well," she said, "who am I? If I were to tell you something about myself I would say that I live not too far from here. You're right about my being a little 'country.' We do try to live more simply now, closer to the land. I'm married, and have been for over fifty years. I have three children. But that probably wouldn't be too interesting to you. Let's see: I like to read a lot, and I'm interested in geology. Out here," she waved her hand broadly over the winding wash and the rocky hillsides, "I feel that I'm really alive." She peered at him. "I suspect you do, too."

"Yes," he said simply.

At last! Here they were, establishing a bit of an accord. She knew, however, that something else was required of her. There was more here than just a "howdy" between strangers passing each other in a canyon on their way to their own destinations. His eyes were wary and watchful, but they revealed a readiness for contact, a need to cast aside convention. He too, seemed to be somehow emboldened by the wilderness. His own inhibitions, like hers, seemed to have vaporized into the grand openness of their surroundings. He could not have planned to do this: to encounter an old woman on horseback and begin a discourse with her on matters of significance. The killdeers had started it. Blame it on the killdeers! What agents God used, Angela thought. St. Augustine had said that not a leaf stirs in a breeze unless it has been willed by God. There was some kind of imperative afoot here.

It was her turn to speak. The Pilgrim was waiting. She took a breath, glanced inward and then upward and hazarded:

"And, of course, there's God."

"Hah!" he said triumphantly, "Just as I suspected: rustic *and* religious!"

"They go together?" she asked.

"Don't they always?"

"Not necessarily." She was looming over him from the back of the horse. It gave her an unfair advantage, she felt. There was a certain power that arose from being, in a group of two, the only one on horseback. She remembered the envy and awe that had once overcome her as a child when she had gazed up at a mounted cowboy. There, indeed, was a god.

LB was still facing back up the wash down which they had come. The low bank was on her left. It was an easy dismount. She got down on the bank then, and leaned across the saddle with her good arm on LB's rump. Her eyes were now more on a level with Pilgrim's.

"Religion has a bad name these days," she said. "It needn't. It's misunderstood and misrepresented. It's not the province of the ignorant and superstitious as people like to say. It's a great adventure, an adventure of the mind *and* spirit. And body." To emphasize the physical she again swept her hand around at the surrounding hills, and gave the horse a nod and a pat. "Religion is not simply 'religious' at all. Or it shouldn't be."

"Religion is not religious. What is it then?"

"I thought you'd never ask!" She laughed. "It's love; it's light; it's being happy. It's searching for and discovering the invisible realities. It's knowing God, really knowing Him. It's trying to do always what He would want you to do." She paused. "Or not doing what He wouldn't want you to do."

"Ah," he said. "Here it comes. Sin."

"You can call it that," she gave him graciously. "But you need to get beyond ideas. God is more than ideas and less than ideas. God made Himself small. He wore a human face. The face of Jesus. Out of the whole universe He chose to make this planet special and to come and live in it." She stopped suddenly at an understanding that was new to her. Should she speak it? Yes. "God never rode a horse," she said wonderingly, mostly to herself. "He never rode a horse, but He *created* horses. Wow…just for us. That's small, and that's big." She realized that he was staring at her more curiously than before. "Plain old human is big, too. Because we're made to be like Him. Aren't you proud to be human? You wouldn't want to be anything less, would you?"

"Certainly *not!*" he said with a slight bow.

She continued as if he had not spoken. "Religion is receiving the gifts that God wants to give you. It's letting yourself be new."

"New. That would be…novel." He laughed shortly.

"It's doable. And it's essential. For all of us. Every day." She gathered up the reins, settling her toe back into the stirrup, hoping she would be able to lift herself into the saddle. Her left leg was getting stiff. "Seek communion," she said. "God is waiting for that with you." She pulled herself onto the horse's back by sheer will power, and waited for the Pilgrim to move on up the wash so she could turn LB and be on her way. She really longed for this conversation to be, finally, over. But still he stood.

"Communion," he said. "I did that once. I did it more than once."

"I'm talking about communion with a small c. You can do that still."

"No. I might be living a 'disordered' life," he said, using a word from the catechism. "No communion for me. Big C *or* small c."

So he had lived, at one time, also a sacramental life. Angela was gripped by this revelation, but she could not bear the thought of getting off the horse again. She leaned over the pommel, resting on her elbows, gazing into his eyes. Wisdom, she groaned silently at the Holy Spirit. Give me wisdom. Show me what the heck you want me to do.

"Have you been Catholic?" she asked.

"Once."

"Then you still are," she said brightly.

"Catholic guilt," he said. "I know about that."

"Catholic conscience," she countered, still leaning toward him across L.B.'s withers. The horse was happy to stand still in the shade. "Conscience is a wonderful thing. That, too, gives us a chance to be more human. What if everyone in the world made an effort to inform their consciences, and then used their reason in exercising them? Don't you think the world would be a better place? And, as for your 'guilt,' there are ways to rid yourself of it. You know about that."

He had been looking down momentarily, but again his head popped up and his eyes caught hers. His alertness was the alertness of a deer: the quick movement of the head, assessment of the situation, watchfulness, and then a return to calm.

Suddenly he laughed. "Did you know my grandmother?" he asked.

She caught his meaning. "I think I do know something about her," she said. The warm brown intelligence of his eyes; the careful precision of his diction; the natural and comfortable reserve that lay behind the present sorrow. It had come from someone, was inbred. And it had been nurtured by someone. She waited for a moment, then added, "I've met *you*."

He understood and accepted the implication.

"Thank you," he said. "She was a lady."

It would be easy, indeed advisable now, for Angela to turn the horse and ride on down the canyon. The man stepped back. She swung L.B. around and started off. She glanced back, to wave. The Pilgrim remained standing where she had left him. The distance between them widened.

Suddenly she turned the horse again and trotted back, stopping in front of him. "Here's something to think about. This isn't me. Not me. This is something the pope said. The old pope. Ready?"

He laughed. "Do I have any choice?"

She tried to remember how it went. "You are not," she quoted slowly, "a being appearing in the world by chance and walking a path toward nothingness." So much for Pope Benedict. He had developed this idea much more thoroughly, but she could not recall all the compelling wisdom of it. So Angela added some words of her own. "You were planned by God from all eternity. He loves you. He intends to love you forever."

She waved again, tentative now, and slightly embarrassed. Then she turned LB and trotted down the wash toward home. How eager she was to get out of here.

9

WHAT WAS ALL THAT ABOUT? She plied herself with questions as they jogged along. What? Where was its meaning? She expected to find explanations for the more startling experiences in her most ordinary life. She had, in fact, a way of demanding those explanations; if not explicit ones, then at least by way of some clue provided from on high. If one looked closely one could usually find a hint of Divine interest or intervention. If nothing else presented itself, one could always blame things on God.

In this particular situation, God had seemed to be hovering nearby, eavesdropping on her confrontation with the Pilgrim, insinuating Himself somewhat into her consciousness, but not favoring her with a single suggestion as to how to proceed. She had ended up feeling simply weak-kneed and hampered by the usual haunting, pervasive societal accusations. The reward these days for any display of moral uprightness was the cry of intolerance, narrow-mindedness, bigotry. You even accused yourself, wondering if you were being prudish for so stubbornly clinging to old-fashioned Christian virtues. Actually, she reminded herself, they were not necessarily Christian virtues, but *human* ones, natural values that adhered to the human race. But these days it was often Christians themselves who promoted or defended aberrant behavior in the name of kindness or modern custom, as if the "loving God" had suddenly changed His mind and was now applauding sin. She wondered whether she herself had been honest enough in the present situation.

She had hardly called a spade a spade in the conversation with the Pilgrim. Had she? If she'd had the moral authority of a St. Thomas Aquinas, she could have used terms such as his: "base passions" and "evil impulses," or, if she'd been courageous, she could have spoken some of her own ideas about the honesty of animals and the comparative purity of their instincts. Instead, she had been cautious, just like everyone else these days.

But she had not been totally timid. Had she, in fact, spoken too freely? What right had she to cast her convictions onto the overburdened psyche of a stranger? However, she had truly been assailed by his need. His need was for real. There he had stood, looking with his deer eyes into her face across the horse's back. She glanced upward, into the heavens. No help from that direction.

It was over, anyway. She would never see him again. And so she prayed. For Pilgrim.

There came to her an image of a bird. She had not thought of it in years, in fact not at all since she had first seen it. But she remembered her reaction to the photograph in those first moments she had gazed upon it. A large sea-bird, a loon or a tern, really quite unrecognizable because of its condition, lay on a towel upon the lap of an intent young woman. The bird was sodden with tar, its feathers welded together. There was no hope for it. Lifeless except for the spark remaining in one eye, it was no longer a creature of sea foam and sky, and would never be again. Still, the young woman had bent over it, wiping it tenderly with a swab drenched in some kind of solvent. Love. That was love. It was all that was required. The bird deserved that last bit of tenderness. She wondered about her own recent motives. Yes, she had to acknowledge that she had felt a movement of pity toward the Pilgrim, an impulse of concern. Was that love? However deficient, it had been there. It had come from her and from beyond her. She said another prayer for him.

LB shied suddenly and stood still. There was rustling in the brush nearby, and Angela expected to see the hound emerge, grinning. Instead, a family of javelinas plunged down the bank onto the sand. LB trembled, but held his ground. She could feel the suppressed power beneath her poised for flight. For a moment they all stood suspended. The javelinas were as surprised as the horse. Apparently they had been moving fast and had not looked before they dashed out of the cover. For a few seconds they milled around grunting and squealing while LB began to dance. Then the two wise mamas began to trot away. The four babies, however, became confused, and hesitated. A boar, large and protective, circled among the young ones. Suddenly two of the babies spotted the mothers crossing the wash and made a dash after them. One of them careened toward LB and ran between his front feet.

Up and up went the little horse, rising high on his hind legs. He became taller than Angela would ever have imagined. She leaned forward over his neck, not wanting to pull him over backward. On his way down his mane ripped through her mouth. He landed with a bounce, and she sat erect and pulled long strands of black mane from between her teeth. The javelinas were now behind them. The horse pivoted to face them, almost throwing her from the saddle. He stood still for seconds only, facing the javelinas, before he began to back rapidly down the wash in the direction of home.

The remaining two baby javelinas fled. Angela managed to hold LB for a moment to stop his backward progress. Watching her, clacking his tusks together and making low growls, stood the male. He stood squarely on legs planted like pillars, his hackles raised. She waited for him to turn and dash after the others, but he maintained his stance and his attitude, and then lowered his head, shaking it like a bull, and made a stiff little lunge at LB. The horse lowered his head, too, and backed farther, still facing the boar. Angela did not want to spin and make a full retreat. She pictured the pig slashing at and reaching LB's back tendons as the horse turned. Or, if they moved fast enough, they would really move, and she would find herself tearing down the canyon on a runaway. If they could only hold their ground now, the javelina would probably lose interest. But he didn't. He advanced again toward them, his jaws open, his long tusks menacing. LB, trembling, continued to face him, moving his feet carefully backward, one at a time. Angela would not let him turn.

Suddenly Zelie appeared on the low bank. She gave a bellow of rage. Then she poised briefly, gathering herself, and launched her body bravely out over the sand in a wide arc, her front legs tucked neatly up under her chin, looking for all the world like a steeplechase champion. Angela would always remember her fine form.

But the leap ended in chaos. The hound blasted herself onto the back of the javelina, knocking it off its feet. For a moment they struggled in the sand, but the pig was quickly up, slashing and lunging. The dog sprang back and then swept in again, now silent and intent. The pig whirled. The horse backed, moving swiftly. Angela had no control over him at all. The reins were useless, except to keep him straight. If she turned him he would bolt. He was bolting now, in reverse. She was astonished by the speed at which he could go backwards. She would have to jump off and let him go, if she wanted to save her dog. How could she save Zelie? But she had to try. She spoke to LB, patting him, trying not to use the reins, which were indeed a temptation. Pulling on them would just propel him backward. She leaned over his neck and kicked at his sides, hoping it would make him think forward. He slowed for a moment and she tightened the reins and prepared to jump down.

In front of them, a hundred feet or so, the hound was down. The javelina rooted at her, snarling. It was only for seconds. Zelie fought her way up and smashed herself into the pig's hindquarters. It staggered and spun on her, snapping.

Angela leapt out of the saddle and left LB behind her, the reins dangling on his neck. She ran, slowly, scrunching into sand, watching for a rock or a good solid branch to use against the enraged javelina.

There was a shout. Here came the Pilgrim from the other direction, running slowly too, because of the sand, but faster than she. He arrived at the battleground first.

Angela stopped. Man, dog, and javelina churned in a savage, snarling, baying, shouting whirlpool. The Pilgrim sprang back and began to lash the pig with his walking stick. The javelina lunged at him, but again Zelie swept in and knocked it off its feet. The javelina then turned on the dog again, rooting its head upward, trying to get under her body. Pilgrim was now dancing and feinting, using his walking stick like a rapier, rushing in at the pig, then springing away. He saw Angela staring, gave her a grin, then assumed a fencer's stance with the stick circling slowly to draw the javelina's attention, and the other arm curving gracefully over his head. The hound paused, watching. Pilgrim leapt forward and retreated, leapt and retreated. The javelina stood, momentarily, puzzled. Then it lunged once more at Pilgrim, knocking the stick aside. But Zelie was upon it and brought it to the ground.

"No!" the man cried. The dog stood back, gasping. The javelina also waited, its sides heaving, growling a little and still snapping its teeth. With great finesse, the Pilgrim directed the drooping hiking pole at the pig's quivering snout, twirling it in small circles. The javelina's small eyes riveted for a moment on the cane. "Touche!" he cried, and catching the pig at the end of its snout, he administered the coup de grace. The javelina gave a final outraged squeal and bolted off across the wash in the direction the others had taken.

Angela stood motionless for some seconds. Zelie was shaking and shaking her head. She seemed to have three ears that were repeatedly wrapping themselves around her skull, clinging for a moment, then freeing themselves and slapping damply back around in the other direction.

She ran to her dog and knelt by her. The Pilgrim hovered nearby. She glanced up at him. His impeccable hiking togs were covered from shoulder to boot with small red droplets. Red raindrops. Blood from the dog's whipping ears.

10

CROUCHING BY ZELIE, ANGELA DISCOVERED A DEEP GASH along her rib cage and some mangled toes. Worst of all, one of her long silky ears was ripped in two, from its base to the tip. Angela started to reach out to it, then dropped her hand. She shut her eyes for a moment against the destruction. There was nothing she could do. When she looked at the dog again a tear slid down her cheek. Zelie's beautiful hound ears. She gathered the good ear into her hand. It was sodden with blood, but it was intact. She reached out again, and this time she did touch the wounded ear, gently. Poor Andrew. The dog stood with her head tipped to one side, the ear dripping. Could it be stitched? Angela wondered if her vet would simply say to leave it alone, that it would eventually heal. In halves. The blood flow was already congealing on the separate parts.

Pilgrim leaned down to examine the gash on the dog's side. "She'll be OK," he said.

And, indeed, Zelie was already limping down the wash to stand by LB. Amazingly, the horse had not bolted away, but had remained near them all, at a distance, watchful.

Angela and the Pilgrim stood still. She looked at him again. He did not appear to be injured, although his walking stick was in a state of serious disrepair.

"Thank you," she said, finally.

"I think I'll call it a day," he said. He turned and walked with her toward the horse.

"Good boy, good *boy*," she praised LB as she reached him and caught the reins. She was a little wobbly. There was no way she could mount immediately, and she had no intention of asking Pilgrim for a leg up. She remained on foot and they continued down the wash, leading the horse. Zelie hobbled along beside them.

They stopped for a minute while Pilgrim took a long drink from his canteen, then poured a little onto a handkerchief to dab on Zelie's wounded side. "She'll be OK," he said again. "This will heal quickly. She might not even need stitches, but it wouldn't hurt." He examined the torn ear carefully. "I don't know if this can be fixed, though," he said sadly. "Don't know about the toes, either. They mostly just look bad, I think, because she's lost a couple of toenails. But let's say she doesn't have any broken bones there." He smiled at Angela.

Angela, watching him swallowing the water, watching as it spread and dampened the handkerchief he held against the dog, found herself swallowing too. Her own throat was raspy dry. Never again would she come out without water. But she would not ask him for a drink. Why? she wondered. Because she was an Angela? She didn't like to ask anyone for anything. Yet earlier she had asked for water for the dog. Why not for herself? Because she had a horror of germs? She had always avoided drinking after other people. Because it was *his* water? No, she could go on without a drink. They walked on. She was still a little shaky.

"What were those things, anyway?" Pilgrim asked.

"Those animals?"

"Yes. I've never seen anything like them."

"Collared peccaries," Angela said, grateful for a neutral topic. "That's their official name, but here in the southwest…" she glanced at him. Where was he from? He was certainly not a local. "Here in Arizona, we simply call them the Spanish word, 'javelinas.' Or pigs. A lot of people think they're wild pigs, but they're not. They sure look piggy, though, with that little piggy snout. And I saw a giant version of them in Texas that they called wild hogs. They must all be related way back somewhere."

"They're savage enough!" he exclaimed.

"Oh, they can be. They can be very savage, especially if they're protecting little ones. They've been known to put hunters up trees. And they can kill dogs. That big one was about to go after my horse. What if I'd fallen off?" She found herself trembling suddenly, remembering the panicky horse, her tenuous perch on his back when he had reared, the urgency she felt in him to spin and run away. And then, the uncontrollable backing. For a moment, her body attuned itself again to the scene of the battle. Her knees became watery with what seemed to be their own private memory of helplessness. They now refused to stiffen themselves for her. She was amazed at their independence. And, against her will, her heart pounded again briefly and then continued threadily. She wanted to sag down into the sand and put her head on her knees, but he was watching, so instead she just stopped walking and bent over the hound, seeking contact. "Zelie saved me, I think." Zelie, at the sound of her name, gave a subdued wag and looked up into her eyes. She was a pitiful looking creature, limping and covered with blood. Angela caught the Pilgrim's eyes. "Zelie kept the pig from us. That was brave of her. And you saved Zelie."

The man said nothing.

Angela straightened her back and asked cheerfully, "But aren't the babies cute?"

"Did you really have time to notice?"

"I've seen lots of them before. Javelinas are like rattlesnakes. You want to leave them alone. They usually just fade away into the brush. This is the first time I've been in a fight with one." She gazed at him steadily. "You saved my dog's life. I do want to thank you again. My husband would have been devastated to lose her. As it is…" she looked mournfully at the tattered ear. "But she's alive, thanks to you."

He nodded politely.

After a pause, it was Pilgrim who picked up the thread of conversation they had long ago abandoned.

"Do you come out here often?" he asked. "All by yourself?"

"No, not often at all. In fact, I haven't been out here in years. I used to hike a lot and I would come here on foot. I used to ride here, too. And then I ran out of horses, and stopped coming altogether."

He looked questioningly at her and then at the horse. "Ran out of horses? Then who is he?"

"My buddy," she said. "Little Big Man. He's not really mine. But in a way, he is. I'm caring for him. He's my last horse."

The Pilgrim reached out a hand and tentatively stroked the glistening copper shoulder. "Why is he the last?"

"You kidding?" She laughed a little snort of a laugh. "Take a look at me."

He did look at her, but for longer than she would have liked, a penetrating look.

"You're a good person," he said finally.

"I wish I were," she said. She had been surprised by his statement, and her own head had popped up, deerlike. Afraid she had now sounded falsely humble, she tried to amend her response. "I do want to be," she paused. "Good." She looked up at him. "I want to." Then, in spite of herself she added, "Don't you?"

"Oh, most certainly," he said. "But how does one do that? What you were talking about earlier, when you left me, that's not for everyone."

"But it *is*," she said. "It *is* for everyone!"

He shook his head sadly.

They plodded along together in the sand. Two strangers, a horse and a dog. Angela once again found her mind reaching out, grasping for something she could lay hold of, something to offer him. Where was this famous Holy Spirit she had heard so much about? She had an urge to look around furtively, to see if there were in fact some semi-visible persona nearby who could be expected to stand in for her. Someone who might relieve her of this unwanted responsibility.

How unfair it was, that she should be faced by this tremendous need from a man who had just saved the life of her dog. That she should have nothing to give him in return. Nothing at all. Certainly no more words.

She decided to ignore the problem for the time being. She had said plenty earlier, she felt. She stretched out her arm and placed her hand on LB's mane, giving his neck an affectionate shake.

For a time they walked on in silence. Then, in spite of her resolution to say no more, she was pierced by an idea that came almost as a command. She tried to shake it off, but it clung to her, relentless. No, she said to herself. Leave it alone. Leave him alone. But there it was, orders from headquarters. Who else was there to do it?

"There can be no such thing as a mute Christian," Pope Francis, had said just recently. Mute! She had not been mute at all so far with the Pilgrim. Was she expected to say more? What was it? She had for verbal resources nothing but her own words springing from her own surprising mental energy. A ruthless energy. In her tired body, her mind began again to dart about like the spark through stubble in the Book of Wisdom, but nothing wise presented itself to her. She was clueless. Still, it seemed something else had to be said. No, mute she could not be. She launched herself again, rather crudely, at the Pilgrim.

"Too bad you're so narrow-minded."

His jaw dropped. The exaggeration in the gesture was only part of it. Angela could tell he was genuinely flabbergasted.

"You're self-righteous, too," she threw in.

"Wait a minute, now," he protested. He stopped and faced her in the wash. They all stopped. LB rested patiently behind them. The dog carefully folded herself onto the sand. "I don't claim that everyone else is wrong, and I'm the only holy one. That's for your crowd. You're the self-righteous."

"See. That's what I mean. You're self-righteous and you don't even know it. Radical social change people are intolerant. They have no use for truth. They make up new rules, or the even happier idea of *no* rules. They want to satisfy themselves, no matter what, and they're determined to have other people agree with them. They have no tolerance for the values of the others."

"But hold on," he objected again. "Radical social change! That's not fair, or even true. At least in my case. I just want to be left alone, to figure things out. I don't impose my ideas on other people."

"The way I see it," she insisted, "you're already being or about to be caught up in a way of living and thinking that is self-destructive and dangerous to society. I've seen this happening. In the movies, in the schools, even in some churches. And people who stand up against it are being ridiculed and intimidated. If we don't go along with it we're accused of carrying around some kind of phobia. Parents are even embarrassed to tell their children that certain kinds of behavior are intrinsically wrong. So, you see..." she paused and chewed on her lip, thinking. Then she smiled and charged on. "There's nothing more self-righteous than the unrighteous when they accuse the righteous of being self-righteous."

"Huh?"

"Think about it. If you uphold moral truths, natural truths, you're considered prudish, simplistic, unkind, bigoted and one step away from being a bully, maybe even a bludgeoner. When, in fact, it is the thoughtful people who are being bullied. A lot. We want to be kind. We live in doubt. Sometimes we even bully ourselves in our own minds."

"Aren't you being a little extreme?"

"Is it extreme to care about your own soul and the souls of others? Souls are important. You only have one, and it can be lost."

"I..." he began.

"You yourself are bigoted," she went on, not waiting for him. She was on a roll! Was she going to regret this later? No doubt. "Don't tell me you don't have a slight prejudice against me. No? Because I'm old? Because I'm a woman? Because you think I'm country-looking? Is it because I dare to say I believe in something that you called me a bumpkin?"

"I never said that!"

"Yes, you did."

"Did not."

"Did too."

"Did not." He laughed. They both laughed.

She was beginning to know him, she thought. And his family. She had already understood that he had been loved by a wise and concerned grandmother. Now it appeared he had also had a problematic sibling. This conversation was reminiscent of the eloquent argumentation of her own children. She decided to try out her theory.

"Did too," she said under her breath.

"Did not," he murmured quietly, getting in the last one. He raised his voice. "And let's be fair. Here is what I said to you: that you seemed like a rustic."

"Should I be insulted?"

"Maybe."

"A religious rustic." Angela was now hopping with laughter and audacity. The horse behind her shifted backward, tightening the reins, and when she turned to look back at him, he fixed big eyes on her. She rubbed his nose. "A religious rustic," she repeated. "The worst kind. Dumb as a post! I have no sympathy or understanding for anyone who doesn't think the way I do. I'm brainwashed by the pope, who is a celibate, understands nothing of human sexuality, and wants nothing for poor oppressed womanhood but that they produce baby after baby to increase the Church's population. Tell me you haven't heard that sort of thing."

"Of course I've heard that stuff. It's stupid."

"But you're wanting to identify with that crowd."

"I am not!"

"You are, too! Tell me you haven't accepted all the propaganda about the horrors of the Spanish Inquisition or the Crusades. You've sympathized with the wonderful native populations who were enslaved by evil missionary priests. Right?"

"Why are you going on like this?"

"Because you need to start thinking again. Some things are true. Some things are totally untrue, or simply exaggerated. You've been under-educated. You've absorbed some truth, but not enough." She had struck a nerve here, she could see. He started to raise an objection, but she gave an emphatic nod and continued. "Deep down in your heart you've nurtured a contempt for my religion. For *your* religion." He moved to object again, but she gave him no chance. "It's true," she said. "You have received that inoculation that Chesterton, or somebody," here she paused, wishing she could remember who had said this. It was good. She went on, a little sobered. "You have been vaccinated against your own religion, against its truth and beauty. You have received and accepted just enough of it, to immunize you against the full power of it. You think you know, or knew, but you didn't. You have joined the ignorant crowd. You are stagnant in the deepest part of yourself."

"Mea culpa," he said, a little wickedly. "You're trying to tell me you're not self-righteous?"

"I'm not," she said. "I'm an ungrateful sinner."

They stood looking at each other for a moment.

"Could I say one more thing?" Angela asked.

"Oh, do," he said.

She opened her mouth, but nothing happened. Not a word emerged. The inspiration had fled. Her battery had fizzled out.

11

SHE HAD WOUND DOWN, EXHAUSTED, DRAINED and incredibly dry of mouth. The Pilgrim had nothing to say. He started to smile at her, but apparently thought better of it. His eyes sought the wash ahead of them. Zelie was reluctant to go on, so Angela took the leash from the saddle pouch and snapped it on her collar. The Pilgrim cautiously took LB's reins from her other hand, keeping a safe distance from the horse's mouth, which he seemed to regard as dangerous territory. They walked silently for a time in the afternoon stillness.

Angela was agonizingly thirsty. All the excitement, the trauma of dangling by one leg from the saddle, the javelina fight, the immense challenge of trying to communicate something to this man, had been too much for her. She had never felt this diminished before. She was desperate to reach the trailer and the water, but walking slowly with the horse was not the best way. When they came to a flat rock in the creek bed, she handed Pilgrim the end of Zelie's leash, took the reins from him and mounted easily. For a short distance they kept together, but of course the horse began to outdistance him.

Angela stopped until he came alongside again. She looked down at him. "I think my dog can come along all right now," she said. "If you'll just unsnap that leash and hand it up to me, we'll go on."

He unhooked Zelie, gave the good ear a rub, and handed Angela the leash.

Suddenly he smiled. "Well, I guess this is goodbye. It's been … nice, talking with you." He smiled again and added magnanimously, "After all, we're all God's children."

"So you've been told." She ignored the goodbye and held back the horse. Her entire purpose in life appeared to be unbefuddling this man. Because he did appear to be befuddled. How could you be a child of God if you didn't want to be a child of God? Did you become a child of God just because you had been born a human being? Jesus had said that to be a mother, brother or sister of his, one had to do the will of the Father. And the Gospel of John proclaimed clearly "But to all who received him, who believed in his name, he gave power to become children of God." You had to believe in Him. What did that mean? Surely that meant you had to think the way He wanted you to think, behave the way He wanted you to behave. It seemed to her that to be God's child involved some choices, some acts of the will. So she spoke to the Pilgrim again, kindly and thoughtfully she hoped. "Actually, we are all God's *creatures*. He created us and He loves us wildly. But to be God's adopted *children* requires a little bit of effort…and grace."

The Pilgrim did not answer.

Her thirst was intense, commanding. No, she had never felt this way before. But once again she was towering above him. He had to tip his head back to look up into her eyes. She kicked her right foot out of the stirrup and dragged her leg back over the saddle to drop to the ground one more time. Would she ever get home? For a moment she leaned against the horse, her head pressed into the leather. What could she possibly do for this man?

"I thirst." One of the last words from the cross. Mother Teresa of Calcutta had the words written on the walls of every one of her convents. "Listen to Jesus' thirst," she had told her spiritual daughters in a letter. "Hear Him." That thirst was meant for every one of them, Mother Teresa had insisted. He thirsted for kinship with every single living soul. For friendship.

Angela lifted her face from against the saddle to turn and look at Pilgrim. He was the one with the water bottle. She tried not to look at it. She was the one with the thirst. She and Jesus. The Pilgrim was not thirsty for water. What did she have that she could give him?

Only the horse.

"Climb on up there," she said. She made a gesture at the saddle. What was she doing? Nobody rode her horse, not even Old Andrew. Once in a while she had been known to boost a grandchild up onto a bare back for a special treat, but that was always a time for hovering. The grandchildren, of course, were always bolder than she would have liked. And she could never tell whether she was more concerned for the welfare of the younger bodies or the older horse. Little Big Man meant a lot to her. He was her last hold on whatever youthful glory she might have once possessed. She stood aside and motioned again for the man to mount.

The Pilgrim was gaping at her. "Go on," she commanded. "The outside of a horse is good for the inside of a man."

"What?" He looked an appeal at her, resisting and determinedly uncomprehending.

"Chesterton," she informed him. "Surely you've heard that old expression." But it couldn't have been Chesterton who said everything. "Or maybe it was C.S. Lewis," she amended. "He liked horses."

Pilgrim was standing stock still, seemingly paralyzed. He looked at the horse and then back at her, shaking his head.

"Winston Churchill!" she said emphatically. "That's it! 'The outside of a horse is good for the inside of a man.' Stop stalling." She gave him a little push to the horse's side and twisted the stirrup toward him. "General George Patton, then," she laughed, as he hesitated.

"The Beatles?" he ventured, buying time. She was relentless. There was to be no escape for him. He raised his left foot finally and stuck the toe of his hiking boot cautiously into the stirrup that Angela held for him. She kept LB still as she guided Pilgrim's left hand to the horse's withers, gave him the reins, and told him how to rise up and swing his right leg over. He did all of this fairly easily, but when he was seated, hunching slightly over the horse's neck, the too short stirrups gave him the look of a crouching monkey. Or a jockey. Or, more precisely, a monkey jockey.

"Don't use the stirrups," she told him. "Take your feet out and just let your legs hang down. Sit up straight. And relax."

"Relax," he said. "Right."

But he straightened, and flexed his elbows a little. She noticed too late that he had kept the broken and dangling walking stick in his right hand. Did he intend to carry it like a lance? Suddenly he looked directly ahead with a little shudder of amazement and discovery. The horse had taken a step. Angela let the Pilgrim keep the pole. She clucked to LB and he moved on. Another few steps, and the horse stopped, turned his head, and looked back at her curiously.

"Go on," she told him. "I'm right here." To Pilgrim, she spoke with assurance, "He'll take you right on down around the bend and to the fence. He'll stop there." She did not add, "I hope." She walked closely beside them for a minute, and then let them go on while she trudged along with Zelie. Around the next bend, she knew, the sagging barbed wire fence crossed the wash. LB would probably stop there for a few minutes. She hoped she would catch up with them before he decided to carry the Pilgrim aside and up the hill, seeking the path they had followed from the trailer. She watched as horse and rider made the turn in the wash and slowly disappeared. The Pilgrim's back was ramrod straight. He did not look back.

12

ANGELA AND THE HOUND STUMBLED ALONG. Zelie's head was down, but in spite of her exhaustion, Angela's head was up. She felt a strange sense of exhilaration but also a touch of trepidation. She wanted to catch a glimpse of her horse as she rounded the bend. What if he had dumped the Pilgrim and thundered off along the fence line for parts unknown. As she spoke encouragingly to the dog she noticed the thickness of her own tongue.

The fence she had crossed earlier came in sight, dropping down the hillside from the left before crossing the wash. And here was Pilgrim, riding back toward her on her own horse. A nice-looking animal, she noticed automatically, irrelevantly. The rider sat tall in the saddle, his long legs dangling, his lance held in the crook of his elbow, a blissful smile on his face, and a faraway look in his eyes. Don Quixote in the flesh. He saw Angela and focused upon her. He rode directly up to her, making a perfect stop, so that LB tucked his head slightly and stood squarely.

"Good job," she said thickly.

"I think you need him." But he continued to sit on the horse, as if reluctant to relinquish him.

Now he was the one looming over her, with the demeanor of a kindly conquistador. It was Angela's turn to look up.

And he looked down. He seemed to have gained a renewed confidence from his exalted stature on the horse's back. He had a question for her.

"I believe you used the term 'human,'" he said. "What if my humanity involved a set of qualities," he seemed to think for a moment, "or maybe only inclinations; yes, inclinations, that were somehow out of the norm? What if this were somehow part of this humanity of mine? Something that was beyond my control and, if I had had a choice would not have been of my choosing? You would have to say *that* was part of God's plan, wouldn't you?"

"Is it?" she asked.

"Is it?"

"Is it beyond your control? Is it part of God's plan? Or if it *is* somehow part of His plan, could it have been meant as a challenge for you? We all have challenges." She was speaking gently to him now, regretting the harshness of her earlier language.

To her surprise, Pilgrim smiled and nodded. "I get your point." he said slowly. "I really do. But...what if, and this is something to think about...what if someone is born a certain way, a way that makes him crossways with traditional morality?"

"Traditional morality. Sounds a lot like conventional morality. I loathe convention. I loathe it!"

"Easy," he said, as if talking to her horse.

She quieted her voice, peering at him. "What if this guy you're talking about really wasn't *born* that way, but that his life experiences, the things that happened to him before he could even remember, or when he was very young, at least, what if he had been influenced by things like that, or things that happened later? What if he had been simply shaped by events or wrong ideas?" She had noticed in recent years the increasing eagerness of the social and news media to promote alternative lifestyles, and even in the public schools the rush to encourage children to make what were now considered brave and happy "choices." She wished now that she could be more articulate. She was beginning to feel a little lame here, knowing that she was opposing herself to much of popular opinion. But still she went on. "And maybe you shouldn't use the word 'traditional.' As in traditional morality. That's kind of numbing. Don't think of it as 'traditional.' Think of it as 'natural.' The natural law. Things as they should be."

"But what if they're not *as* they should be?"

She had only one card left to play. "Then self-control. A virtue always in season. It's required of all of us."

And, once again and at last, she had nothing more to say. He sat on her horse, looking down at her.

"I thirst." She understood the thirst of Jesus. She understood Pilgrim's own thirst. No, his was not a thirst for water. But she had nothing more to give him. Definitely, she decided, no more words. Pilgrim was the one with the canteen. She was the one who needed water. "I thirst," she could have said for herself, but she would not. Why not? Pride? The Samaritan woman at the well had given Jesus to drink, but He had told her that had she only realized, *He* was the one offering the life-giving water. And yet truly Jesus had thirsted then, and again on the cross. Even now He thirsted. For the heart and soul of every world-weary pilgrim. Jesus was not proud.

"Take the horse," Angela said. "Ride on down to the fence again. I'll be along in a minute." She reached up for the hiking pole and he disarmed himself obediently.

Her boots dragged heavily in the sand. She wanted to give him more time with LB and, as it turned out, it was going to take her a lifetime to reach the fence. She could see him at the barricade up ahead. He stopped squarely at the fence, another good stop, then turned to the right along the line, made a complete circle and reversed himself along the strip of wire and tangled brush. He turned to face her, giving a triumphant little wave. She staggered a little, hoping he didn't see. She would have leaned on the walking stick, had it not been useless. Zeli, who was infamously unruly on a leash, was by this point a paragon of heeling obedience without one. She followed slowly, the tips of what were now three long ears dragging in the sand. If the OA could only see us now, Angela thought.

When she finally reached the fence line Pilgrim had already dismounted and was handing her the reins.

"He's all yours again," he said. "Thank you." He turned and ran his hand along LB's sleek haunch.

"What did I tell you? The outside of a horse *is* good for the inside of a man!"

"T.S. Elliot," he ventured, making a little face.

"Right."

They laughed.

"You love beauty." Angela smiled at him. And then she could not resist adding, "You cannot also love ugliness."

The way for the horse and her led to the right, a shortcut she remembered, through thick brush and to a narrow wire gate against the opposite hillside. She knew the dog could find her way through and back to the trailer on her own. The fence here in the wash was low, dragged down by flood wrack. She could see by his tracks that Pilgrim had crossed here on his way up. He could cross it again easily. It was time, at last, for them to separate.

"You're thirsty," Pilgrim said.

"Yes. But I'll be OK. I have water back at the truck." She ran her sleeve over her face, and when she looked at him again he was extending the canteen toward her.

"Take it."

Springs of life-giving water.

"No. Thank you anyway."

He continued stretching the canteen out to her. Smiling.

I thirst.

Angela thought again of the thirst of Jesus, of His humility at the well as He accepted water from the woman whose own need was greater than his own. She thought again of His tremendous need on the cross. His thirst, yes, but greater still, the yearning of His loving, merciful heart that longed eternally to spill the fountain of life-giving water that could not be pent up in Him.

She had let the Pilgrim ride her horse. That was not enough. She needed to humble herself even more before this creature for whom a

God had died. The Pilgrim was sacred. The most generous and merciful thing she could do would be to share his water.

She reached out shakily and took the canteen from his hand.

13

As she drank, the light changed. The sunshine and shade in which they had been standing became a fountain of purest radiance. The light poured down over her like water, while it seemed to rise up around her from the earth. More than light. It was a fountain of fire with the liquidity of water. Quenching. Her thirst was slaked. Her heart was eased. Light and more light. Pilgrim stood in it, too. They were both awash in it. He stood as if he were listening to something, looking inward. The self that was Angela's own separated from her and stood apart. She seemed to gaze at her soul. It was not her mind. It was nothing she remembered.

Springs of living water. Perfect light. A purifying fire. She and Pilgrim exchanged glances in a recognition of shared astonishment. They had no need to speak of it. They were caught in it. It had touched each of their souls distinctly and was still embracing them. Separately. Differently. Still, for a moment, it held them bound to each other, knowing each other. He stared at her. What was he seeing? Her own eyes seized upon his profound humanity, his pain, God's knowledge of him, so much deeper than her own understanding. How much God loved him.

Stillness held them there for a moment, suspended, and then the ordinary stillness descended, the quiet of an April day, the drone of afternoon insects. The shade-mottled sunshine returned to the floor of the canyon. The horse, drowsy, appeared to have noticed nothing.

Angela and the Pilgrim stood, wrapped in something they could not for the moment shake away.

Was it the same for both of them? She wondered. But no, it couldn't have been. Her history, her entire being, had been known by Someone. She had witnessed Pilgrim being known, and not by her. Known and knowing.

Now they stood face to face again, alone, in simple daylight. Silent.

She handed the bottle back to him. "Thank you." How strange it seemed to say that. Only that. And then she gave him the broken walking stick. She shook her head over it. "Sorry." They gazed at each other again for a long moment. "You can go right across here." She pointed to the fence. "I see you did it already. But the horse and I will have to crawl through those mesquite thickets to get to our gate. You'll probably get back to your car before I get there."

She was, suddenly, very shy. "Well," she said. "Goodbye." She wanted to say more to him, but was seized, acutely, with a sense of the vanity of language. "Well," she said again. Their eyes locked on each other's briefly. She held out her hand humbly and he took it.

"Friends?"

She was surprised. "Yes," she replied. "Yes. Friends."

She turned and led LB up the low bank, ducking under a drooping branch of mesquite into the density of thorn.

Mystery, she thought. Already the profusion of luminosity in which they had just stood was beginning to seem unreal to her. Had she only imagined it? Or was it part of a reality that was more real than the sweaty animal who followed her so closely through the tangle of brush that reached out for them. She was having to watch out for the two of them, pick the route that accommodated his height and bulk. LB kept his head down and was wise and calm enough to duck when he needed to, but she was concerned about her good saddle and her fairly new shirt. *This* was the real world, then, wasn't it? This present life that became a thicket, with its constant demand for watchfulness. With the inescapable thorniness of the immediate, the ensnarement of the consciousness in the here and now. There was no ethereal light now to guide her through. Were the thorns and snags more powerful than the light had been? More real? She wrenched her hair free from the grip of a reaching juniper branch. She wondered what the Pilgrim was thinking. She wished that for him, at least, the moment in the radiance would endure.

A bird made a shrill call and swept out of the brush beside them, looping ahead of them through the branches. She caught the brief flame flash of color under his wings and the white brilliance above his tail, and then he vanished. There was a glow at her feet. She stooped to pick up a feather. Red-shafted flicker, of course, but it wasn't red-shafted at all. The feather she held was warmest peachy salmon along the shaft and all the way out to its coaly edges, where it was sprinkled with purest white. A work of art. LB reached from behind and nudged her shoulder with his nose. She tucked the feather behind her ear and they moved on and came out of the brush and shadow into the clearing before the wire gate. Zelie had gone on ahead.

The gate was in sunshine. She dropped the reins and struggled with the barbed wire loop. When she led LB through and rewired the gate she stood for a moment in the demanding light of day, her head bent down against his shoulder. They had truly returned to her world of fact and necessity. She heard the *scree* of the flicker again and then his *wika-wika-wika*. She made her own *wika-wika-wika* as best she could, mimicking him, looking for him. It turned out he had crossed to her side of the fence now and was hopping up the trunk of a piñon tree with his woodpecker toes, balancing himself with his beautiful tail. He peered at her, assessing her *wika*. Not quite right. She was a phony, he thought. He hopped sideways around the trunk until he disappeared. From the other side of the tree, he peeked out cautiously to scrutinize her once more. She caught a glimpse of the red stripe along his cheek and the bold black shield upon his breast. Then off he swooped, flashing brilliant salmon in the very real sunlight.

Words from a Hopkins poem came to her. They were the final lines from "God's Grandeur," the same poem she had once quoted to

Windwhisper and Mr. P. in that other canyon. It seemed like a bizarre dream now, that unique threesome of strangers huddling around a campfire. Three strangers and a dog. What had possessed her, to recite poetry in such a perilous situation? The lines she had chosen to pronounce to them at that time were different from the ones that claimed her now. Why, suddenly, were these concluding lines reaching out for her? She had a strange relationship with Gerard Manley Hopkins. Sometimes his poetry was problematic and obscure for her, but always, it seemed, he was there with a wonderful word or an image. A Jesuit, he seemed to have a profound infusion of the Holy Spirit. Fire and light one saw in his poetry. Life and little things. Personalities. A fresher vision. It seemed Hopkins had given her that gift once again, as the bird flew away, leaving her with the tag end of her Cottonwood Basin poem:

"Because the Holy Ghost over the bent World broods with warm breast, and with ...ah! bright wings."

Bright wings. She thought of the Holy Ghost, the Holy Spirit, as the dove brooding over the bent world. A mother dove brooding with warm breast. Birds were wonderful metaphors. She thought of her own canyon wren again, of its rapturous song; of the determined broody mother killdeer and her brave and clever tactics to protect her shallow nest; of the jay that had made his brief, blue appearance this morning in the tree beside the dog, the horse and her. Of the flaming wings of the flicker. Birds, but more than birds. Bright wings they had. And all of them, like Shelley's Lark, came "from Heaven or near it." The blackened sea bird whose photograph had distressed her. Even its wings might be bright again someday. Would birds go to Heaven? Would she? She had blackened and defaced her own wings, her own soul, many times over the years.

Bright wings over the bent world. Bent it was. Bent and suffering was the world from which she and Pilgrim had sheltered for a tempestuous time in this peaceful canyon. When she led LB through the gate she had walked back into that bent world. Deliberately. But they had known the bright wings, as well. She and Pilgrim.

14

The Pilgrim was at the parking area when she arrived, leaning over, arranging things in his car. The hound was late. Angela untacked her horse, left him tied to the trailer, and had another drink from the canteen in the truck. She was used to waiting for dogs, and had a supply of reading material, including her breviary. Her treasure. What a gift for the Church the breviary was, this official book of prayers, the Liturgy of the Hours. Psalms and biblical passages and meditations from the saints, all arranged according to the days and seasons...and hours. A way to praise and petition God in His own words. Aside from her own spontaneous prayers, she was grateful for this way of joining other believers all over the world in a common purpose. Zelie was taking her time returning. Perhaps she would give Angela the chance to pray the Office of Readings. She longed to take a few minutes now to pray the psalms out loud, as she often did when she was alone. She waited for Pilgrim to drive away, but he didn't. He sat in the car. Was he, too, waiting to see the hound show up? She gave him his privacy and opened her book, settling herself on the tailgate of her truck to pray silently. In minutes Zelie trotted slowly in. Angela replaced a ribbon, shut the book and stooped over her. A sorry specimen she was. And yet the Pilgrim was right. The dog would survive. She gave Zelie water, and decided to let her into the trailer's tack compartment for the ride home. It would be heartless to ask the hound, bruised and stiffened as she was, to try and jump up into the back of the truck.

And suddenly, out of nowhere, a breeze. It riffled through the lightweight pages of the breviary she had left on the tailgate, displacing all the ribbons and scattering her collection of holy cards. Desperately, she tried to race after them, but she was sore and awkward, and it was too late. Pilgrim ran too. He jumped out of his car, pursuing the cards as they fluttered across the parking lot. She had managed to capture some of them, and he came to her with a few others clutched in his hand.

"Thank you." She laughed. "It seems I have to say that to you a lot." She stuffed the cards behind the front cover of the book, along with the disarranged ribbons. She could deal with them all later.

Horse and dog loaded, Angela made a wide circle with the truck and trailer and pulled out for home. She had to pass close to the Pilgrim's car. He was seated behind the wheel again, looking at something he was holding. He started to raise it up toward her, but apparently changed his mind. Instead, he simply lifted his head to acknowledge her as she crept slowly by. She rolled down her window and leaned out to look down at him. She had to look way down. The red car was unbelievably low slung. Again she was looming over him. He peered up at her.

"Get a horse!" She shouted it cheerfully down at him, wondering if he had ever heard that old country saying. He grinned. She raised her hand in a gesture of farewell, and he raised his, too, but in a signal to stop her. She braked again and looked down at him, waiting.

"Will Rogers," he said.

She squinted at him, awaiting the clarification. "What?" she had to ask finally.

"The outside of a horse is good for the inside of a man."

"Oh. Yes!" She nodded. "Yes. *That's* where it came from. Will Rogers. I see you're a bit of a bumpkin, too." He ducked his head in humble acquiescence, and she laughed and started to drive on.

He raised his hand again for her to stop. She waited. Once more, he looked up into her eyes, persistently.

"Sad," he said, and nodded decisively. He meant it. It was a concession, an acknowledgement of what she had told him earlier. Yet the eyes were not deeply sorrowful, as they had been before.

She left him there.

15

WHEN SHE ARRIVED HOME ANDREW WAS IN THE KITCHEN. She had already turned LB out and watched him roll. She walked by the kitchen window and tried to catch the OA's attention to wave at him, but he was bustling. A good sign. She might not have to cook. She went on in.

"You're a little later than I thought you would be," he told her over the cutting board, though not accusingly. "Was he a good boy?" Meaning LB.

"Oh, yes!" she said enthusiastically.

"Are you limping?"

"Not really."

"Ah." He continued mincing an onion. "Were you able to get on and off?"

"Only about a hundred times."

"You'll have to tell me all about your adventures."

He always said this. It sometimes took her a day or two to give him, in dribs and drabs, all the details that he delighted in hearing. This time she had plenty of stories. It would take days and days to tell all she had to say. She hoped to begin with the news of Whisper and then go on to Dr. Malcom J. Mackenzie. They had both known Dr. Mackenzie in their student days. Andrew had heard her description of the hackberry's resemblance to the good professor. She had taken him once, on foot, to view the tree, and he had to agree with her. That was a Malcolm J. Mackenzie tree if there ever was one. He would be sad to hear the hackberry had disappeared. Yes, they would have a lot to discuss this evening.

But "Where's the puppy?" he asked.

"Getting a drink." Angela screwed up her courage. It had to be told. She gave him a brave smile. "Zelie has a badge of honor."

The next day, Zelie lay on her cushion in the back of Andrew's truck, drugged, stitched and subdued. The vet had been able to sew her ear together and had put a few precautionary stitches in her side.

"This is never going to be glamorous," he said about the ear. "But if the cartilage holds, she'll end up with only two ears again."

Two ears. Not three. Good for Zelie.

Bringing her back from the clinic, they noticed a couple of Department of Public Safety helicopters batting up and down the river, following its course through town, then swinging low out over the fields and subdivisions.

"Must be another escapee," Andrew said.

They laughed. Recently a series of inmates had wandered away from the county jail north of town, providing entertainment for the locals and embarrassment for officials. But these happy hitchhikers had usually been caught within hours. There had been no helicopters.

"This must be a big one," Angela guessed.

Fairly early on the following morning they could hear the rhythmic, persistent thumping of a helicopter approaching their own place. Their cottonwood's leaves trembled beneath its passage before it swung north and the sound of the throbbing receded.

"I hope there's not a child missing," Angela said.

It had taken some time for Angela to recount her adventures to Andrew, and she still wasn't through. Zelie had taken a lot of their attention.

But Zelie was not the only casualty.

"I guess I'll never find my card again," she said sorrowfully to Andrew. She had carried the holy card with her for years, marking a section of her breviary. It had belonged to her mother, who did not remember where it had come from. A relative, probably. Someone in the family had been in trouble, apparently, at some remote point in time. The card, tattered and faded, bore a picture of San Patricio Monastery in New Mexico. "Come to me," it invited under the picture, "all you who are weary and heavy laden…" The monastery was famous for being a place of refuge. For years San Patricio had provided a temporary, and sometimes a permanent, home for men seeking solace or rehabilitation. Angela liked to gaze at the angled watercolor of this sanctuary with its blue wooden gate and the bougainvillea draping the adobe walls. When her own life got a little tattered, she would sometimes picture herself inside those walls, all alone, not a monk or any other man in sight, tending a little garden and a herd of goats, with a cat for conversation. The psalm on the back of the card, Psalm 130, sometimes said it all for her, expressing her own plea: "Out of the depths I cry to you, O Lord. Lord, hear my prayer." *De Profundis.* "Out of the depths."

But now the card was missing. The wind gust at the Cherry Creek parking lot had carried it away, probably into the brush, and it had not been retrieved with the others. She and Andrew had driven out to look for it, to no avail. And even today, though Andrew had kindly rearranged all the ribbons in her breviary for her, and the other cards were tucked neatly back in their places, still she had yearned for the adobe walls of San Patricio and Psalm 130 as she and Andrew had said the morning prayers together.

Now they were lingering over breakfast. They had spent a lot of time at that old table over the years. Conversation had held their family there many times when chores and homework had needed to be done. These days, when it was only the two of them, they still dawdled over the scarred wood sometimes, just chatting.

Suddenly Angela spied a head passing the kitchen window.

"Hey," she exclaimed, "a policeman!"

"A deputy," Andrew corrected.

"Oh, he's from the county?"

"No, just one of our local boys. From the Marshal's Office. They like to call themselves Deputy Marshals."

"But it looks like Jack Vada's son."

"It is."

"But *he's* not a deputy!"

"Where have *you* been?"

"My gosh." She sat stupefied.

"Let him in anyway," Andrew said.

Sure enough, the man introduced himself as Deputy Dusty Vada. She had not seen him for some time. He appeared to remember Andrew and her somewhat, and he gave them a curt, deferential acknowledgement without mentioning their sons. He was not the awkward teenaged boy that she recalled from a last encounter. He carried a clipboard, a holstered pistol, and a businesslike expression.

He joined them, without much urging, at the breakfast table, although there was nothing left to eat. Angela poured coffee, wishing she had doughnuts to offer. They themselves never ate doughnuts, but Dusty, slightly soft, looked as if he might have downed many, glazed and unglazed. Maybe even chocolate covered. Andrew had told her that was what policemen did. And of course the OA knew who was a policeman or who was a deputy. Or who was all grown up, had three kids, and was now a volunteer for the fire department. He acquired a lot of news about the community on his visits to the post office. Sometimes it took him thirty minutes to pick up the mail, depending upon what fellow citizen he ran into.

Of course Dusty had come on official business, and he got right down to it.

"There's a man missing," he said.

"Someone escape from the jail?" Angela could see that Andrew had caught himself just in time. He had been about to say, *again*?"

"No. A big shot. Some kind of consultant for the town. A visitor. I think they said he was an architect." He chuckled. "Now why would this town need an architect? We got all the buildings we need, and then some." He shook his head, looked at them for agreement, and then got back to business. "Missing three days now. Went out hiking and never came back. Found his car down by the river."

"Why..."Andrew began, but Angela had a sudden insight. She cut him off.

"I know why, Honey," she said. "He's the one. The man I met in the wash. He must be. I've never seen him before, or anyone like him. He sure wasn't from around here." She turned to the deputy. "That's why you've come, isn't it? Did you think I might know something about him, the man you're looking for?"

Deputy Dusty Vada nodded solemnly. "Maybe."

"I did see a man," she went on, trying to be helpful, "and he must be the man you're looking for. I think I know who he is. Or no, I don't actually. I don't know his name."

"We know his name," Dusty said significantly.

"Did he have a red car?"

"Yeah. A red Corvette." He glanced at Andrew.

Andrew sighed. He rubbed his hand tiredly over his face and looked sideways at Angela. "Can this be happening..." and this time he did say it... "*again?*"

"No, Honey," she told him emphatically. "This time it's different. But I'm sure he's the man I told you I ran across in Cherry Wash, the one who saved Zelie." She turned to Dusty. "Why is he missing? What happened to him?"

"We were hoping you could tell us." Dusty said dryly, addressing his clipboard. He sounded almost like an investigator from an old TV show.

"Of course you were," Andrew said, equally dryly. And then he asked sternly, "What does my wife have to do with this?" Andrew sounded like a TV husband from the same show.

Angela turned to him. "I did talk with him quite a bit." She had not told Andrew about her entire conversation with Pilgrim. The encounter had ended up being something sacred. Unexplainable. The deputy didn't need to know everything, either. She herself did not understand all that had happened that day. She was still sorting it out. But something was required of her now. She must be as helpful as possible, but careful language was called for in this situation. "He has to be a man I met when I was riding," she said to the deputy. "He was so obviously a stranger here, and he had that funny little car." She mused for a minute. "Yes, I spoke with him, but how did you know that?"

"Funny little car," Dusty was saying wonderingly.

"A nice looking little car, actually," Angela amended. "And not that little, actually."

"Nice looking," Dusty said. He winced dramatically, and then with another chuckle he actually wrote the words on his clipboard, pronouncing them distinctly. "Nice looking little car." He then gave a subdued laugh, not quite as subtle as before; and with a slight flourish he underlined them.

He spoke to Andrew then, directly, and with a carefully expressionless face. "It was a Corvette, like I told you." He paused a moment. "The new Stingray."

"Oh," Andrew said. He declined to give Dusty the knowing glance he was expecting.

"How did you know I had seen him?" Angela insisted. She was suddenly in anguish. "Do you think he's all right?"

"Eddie was out there at the parking lot." He seemed to think they knew Eddie. Maybe they did. Another almost-contemporary of their own boys? "Checking for vandals," he went on. "We've had some little scum bags messing around out there."

Andrew gave Angela another glance. It was beginning to look like she would never visit Cherry Wash again. Not in her lifetime!

"Eddie saw the Stingray," Dusty was going on, "and your truck. Got your plates. Just routine. But...," he said reflectively, "it's strange. I wasn't on the force at the time, but I do remember something you was involved in before. Aren't you the one had the run in with that loser out in Cottonwood Basin? Killed him?"

Angela could feel Andrew swelling and bristling beside her. She smashed his toe with her foot.

"No. I didn't kill him. He fell. Remember?"

The deputy rubbed his chin. "I do remember. I do remember. Sure. He fell." He paused. "But you helped." He paused again. "Well, no great loss to the world, anyway." He clicked his pen, readying it. "Now, what are you going to tell me about this other guy? This Cherry Wash guy."

Angela had been listening to her heart turning over. Had she helped "Mr. P." to die? Strange; the man she and Windwhisper had called Mr. P. had, as it turned out, actually *been* a Mr. P., a Mr. Craig Pearson. He had been a man with a name, after all. She had been trying to save Whisper and herself from Mr. P., trying hard. But had she killed him? Over the last couple of years she had not blamed herself. Too much. But had she done enough for him after he fell? She still wondered.

Andrew had been sitting quietly, but Angela did not need to look at him to know that he was still bristling, bristling. She was reminded of the spikey ridge along the javelina's back.

She laughed disarmingly at Dusty. "Of course, I realize that you *know* I didn't kill him, officer." The word felt foreign on her tongue. She had never said it before. She had never known anyone she could call officer. *Was* he an officer?

The OA shifted in his chair, and Angela saw the corners of his mouth twitch. Maybe Dusty Vada was not an officer. But he must be something. He had several impressive patches sewn on the chest and sleeves of his uniform. Perhaps they were significant. She resolved to give Dusty his proper dignity at the next opportunity.

"Well, anyway," Dusty was saying, "he killed more people than you ever done."

"True," Angela agreed mildly. She carefully avoided catching Andrew's eyes. Their own children, who had attended the same public schools as Deputy Vada and were now scattered here and there about the world, at times caused her to worry. But could they possibly be proceeding through life with such bravado? No. "Tell me about this man you're looking for, Sergeant," she prompted Dusty.

Andrew gave a strangled cough.

Dusty snapped his eyes around at him suspiciously.

"Phlegm," Andrew said.

Dusty questioned Angela with his eyes.

"Phlegm," she nodded in corroboration. "That's f-l-i-m," making it easy for him, thinking for a moment he was going to write it down as a point of official exactitude.

He declined. Instead he said, "Tell you about him? Not much to tell. We don't know that much ourselves. Probably wasting our time, anyway. It's my opinion he's a suicide, but of course, I don't know everything."

"Of course not," Andrew agreed heartily.

Dusty, determined, went on with his deputy work. "I still need to know what you seen out there. How long did you talk to this guy?"

"As I told you, I did talk to him quite a bit," Angela said carefully, thinking. How much did he need to know? She made a decision. "He was hiking up Cherry Wash and I was riding. He helped me with my dog when she got into trouble with some javelinas. Then I spoke with him again back at the parking lot." She did not want to reveal too much about her various conversations with Pilgrim. She was not particularly proud of them. "That was the last time I saw him."

"So he made it back to his car. Was he alone?"

"Oh, yes. When I left, he was still there, sitting behind the steering wheel, but I had the impression he was about to leave."

"Behind the wheel," Dusty said as he wrote. He glanced at Andrew. "That wheel is covered with leather. Real leather. Cow hide. The seats are covered with leather."

Angela thought back to her last good view of Pilgrim. She remembered the discomfort she had felt as she leaned from the truck window, the same sensation she had known on the horse's back; that she was towering over him, assuming a dignity she did not have or did not want to possess. He had sat encapsulated in crimson glory, the low slung car all potential power and velocity; yet he himself had appeared vulnerable and very much alone; and even the car, with its coating of dust and its closeness to the rutted earth, seemed to speak a language of dreary insufficiency.

"Describe that car again to me," Dusty said. "I want to make sure we're talking about the same one."

"What I saw was a red sports car," Angela said, trying to be specific. "A fancy one. I thought it was awfully long, but maybe that's because it was so very, very low."

"The new Corvette Stingray," Dusty said again. He looked incredulously at Angela like this was something she should have known. "They just came out with it. They haven't called one a Stingray since 1976."

"Were you born then?" Andrew asked.

"Oh, and it had those fancy spoke wheels," Angela kept on. "No, not spoke, either. They weren't spindly and aluminum looking like others I've seen. They were black bars. Just a few of them. Stronger looking. Interesting." She was proud of this proof of observation.

"Interesting," Dusty echoed. He did not write this down. Looking at Andrew, he gave a litany of the car's attributes. "455 horsepower; 6.2 liter V-8. You can have either 6-speed automatic or 7-speed manual transmission. This one had the manual. Seven forward speeds! Brembo brakes." He paused dramatically.

"Cool," said Andrew. Angela recognized the brief droop at the corner of his left eye as a wink at her.

"But where is it now," Angela demanded. "Where is *he*?"

"The Stingray is down by the river. We don't know where he is. Could be he's in the river."

They were all very quiet for a moment.

16

ZELIE WAS SITTING PRIMLY NEARBY, her front feet planted together in purebred hound form and her hindquarters gathered compactly under her body. She would have looked beautiful, except that she had a large plastic cone around her head to protect her wounded ear from her scratching. Beautiful, indeed, she still was, but comical in her clown ruff. The deputy studied the dog for a moment and then looked away without making a comment.

"An accident?" Angela finally asked.

"Where? Oh, you mean that guy. Nah. He's in the river. Suicide."

"No, I can't believe he would have done that."

"What would he have done, then?"

"Maybe he's just been walking along the river. He's quite a hiker."

"Well he went off without his hat, then. We found it right by the water. And the car was parked nearby, unlocked. Keys in it. People have been calling, looking for him. It don't make sense." He peered at her. "And…he left a note. Strange one. Said his sister could have the car. Almost sounded like he wanted to get rid of it! But didn't make no mention of wanting to end it all. End it all. That's what they all say. Not him." He fixed Angela with a deputy stare. "Now, there was also some folks who thought they seen him walking south, along the river, toward the freeway. What would you think of that? You have to keep in mind they was hippies, though."

"Did he have his walking stick?" Angela played for time. She had no idea *what* she thought.

"Yeah, he had a hiking pole, for what it was worth. They said it was busted, and he was just carrying it. He had on fancy matching clothes; lots of straps and pockets. Covered with what looked like blood, though. Did you see that?"

"Yes," she said. "But it wasn't his own blood. It came from my dog." She took a few minutes to tell Dusty the entire javelina story. "So that's where the blood came from," she finished, "and why the walking stick was broken." She looked at Zelie. "And why she's wearing the cone. She may have saved my life. And he may have saved hers."

"Wonder why he kept that pole," Dusty snorted. "Kept it and not the Corvette."

"Badge of honor," Andrew put in. "He saved the hound."

Dusty remained unimpressed by the hound and javelina saga. He went on cheerfully, suddenly directing the deputorial inquisition at Andrew.

"Tell me this," he asked him, "meaning no disrespect, of course." He pointed at Angela, "Do you always let her go out riding alone?"

"We have only one horse now," Andrew said.

"One horse might be one too many. We'll be out looking for *her* one of these days." Dusty peered significantly at Andrew.

"It hasn't happened yet."

"There's always a first time. And when we find her, *if* we find her, it won't be pretty. You got no control over her?"

"Never have."

"I wouldn't have one like that!"

"You married?"

"No."

"Then you wouldn't know. I got no choice." Andrew sounded a bit like the deputy.

Angela felt a pang of remorse. She had told Andrew all the details of the javelina attack, how LB had reared and Zelie had distracted the boar while Pilgrim had rushed in to rescue Zelie. But she had not told Andrew about the earlier precarious dangling over LB's back. That could have been the end for her. Andrew didn't deserve to have his wife die in a grisly accident. He was still troubled over what she had gone through those few years before, in Cottonwood Basin. She had been saved once, in a canyon, *by* a canyon; apparently *for* a canyon. Here she was, just recently, again in a canyon. And again, it seemed, having another close call. A couple of close calls, in fact. Another encounter with a stranger. *And* possibly a mystical experience. Maybe she really should just stay home from now on. Hit the rocking chair and pick up the knitting needles.

Dusty had turned away from Andrew and was looking at her speculatively, as if he might read her thoughts.

But Andrew wasn't finished yet. The conversation had gotten a little earnest and he did like to lighten things up a bit. He seized Dusty's attention with a throat clear and then began to hum a few bars. When he felt confident with the tune he began to sing. "She might've been a headache, but she never was a bore." He sang it as best he could, and boldly.

Dusty snickered a little, but silenced himself when he saw Andrew still looking at him.

"Thanks for the Memories," Andrew informed him.

"You're welcome," the deputy replied with sincerity. In the silence that ensued, he glanced quickly at Andrew again.

"That was a song," Andrew said.

"Never heard of it."

"I know."

"Many's the time that we feasted," Angela sang helpfully, giving Dusty a clue and Andrew a reproachful glance.

"And many's the time that we fasted," from Andrew. And then they both chimed in together: "But all in all, how our love lasted." They looked at each other. "We did have fun..."

Andrew dropped out, racking his memory, but Angela carried on: "...and no harm was done." But then she too dropped out, taking a kindly notice of Dusty's silence.

But Dusty apparently had decided to join in the fun. "No harm!" he exclaimed. "What about that guy you killed in Cottonwood Basin?" The deputy did cling to his ideas.

Andrew and Angela laughed heartily, and Andrew reached over and clapped Dusty on his insignia. "You're single-minded, Deputy," he said. "I'm glad to see a man so dedicated to duty."

"Well," the deputy drawled, clearing his throat humbly. He looked at Angela. "I guess you don't know much else. Did this guy seem to be depressed? I always got to ask this."

Angela remembered the sorrow in the Pilgrim's dark eyes, but she also remembered the embracing light, real or imaginary, that they had stood in. She recalled the last view she had of him, peering up at her from the car, when he had admitted, finally, that he was unhappy. Yet there had been a certain grim humor lurking at the corners of his mouth.

"No," she answered. "Not depressed."

"Well, that's about it." Dusty rose to leave.

"Please," Angela begged. "Do let us know what you find out about him."

"You can call. Or read about him in the paper. We'll find him. Some day."

They remained planted in their chairs and let him depart without ceremony.

When they saw that the official head had safely passed the kitchen window, and the deputy was indeed going back toward the front gate, they looked at each other numbly. Andrew leaned back in his chair and shut his eyes.

"Oh!" Angela exclaimed. She jumped to her feet. "I didn't get that man's name. Why didn't I think of asking?" She started to run for the door to go after Dusty, but Andrew stopped her.

"Leave it," he said. "You'll find out soon enough. You can't possibly want to have another conversation with him at the gate. Life's too short."

"We need to pray for him."

"We sure do. But not right now. I don't want to even think of him."

"I mean the Pilgrim. We need to pray for him."

"The pilgrim?"

"Yes. Pilgrim. The man from the canyon. That's what I call him in my mind."

"Pilgrim." He looked up at her from under his eyebrows. "Another Mr. P. Do we need this?"

"This is different."

"Have you told me everything?"

"There's more to tell," she admitted. "And I *will* tell you. But he's not a Mr. P. He's...a pilgrim."

He caught her studying him and smiled at her, trusting her. "Sure, we can pray for him. We don't need to have his name."

"We should pray for his parents."

"Pilgrim's?"

"No. Dusty's. I remember Jack and Elsie Vada as being really nice. Especially Elsie. This must be hard on them."

Andrew laughed. "And you wondered if your own kids were becoming rough stones!"

"Oh, no. Our children are beautiful."

"Well, this experience has been good for you in some ways, at least."

"But, how terrible," she insisted. "I haven't seen them in years."

"Our children?"

"No. Jack and Elsie."

"They moved away."

"I don't blame them." She reflected for a moment, remembering the quiet woman who had helped with catechism classes, and who could always be counted on when people were in need at the parish.

Her husband, Jack, had been more boisterous. Dusty had been their only child, and she remembered him, but somehow as having a different name. Since he was younger than her own children she had not seen the boy much in later years, and not in church either, it suddenly occurred to her. She pondered the problem of his name. Surely it had not been Dusty. She would have remembered that. But for the moment she could not come up with anything better. Later. Things often came to her later. Jack and Elsie, though. She could remember them clearly. But they had dropped from sight and she had not thought about them for some time. "They must be as old as we are," she reflected out loud. "They've got to have one foot in the grave, too."

"Jack does. Elsie has both feet in the grave."

"No!"

"Where *have* you been? I've known that for quite a while."

"I don't go to the post office."

17

ANGELA WOKE ABRUPTLY FROM A SLEEP or a dream a few nights later. *Was* it a dream? Her eyes looked clearly beyond the darkness into a definite distance. At the end of the distance there was light, a somehow familiar light. A light bringing knowledge. She lay still for a moment and then seized Andrew's shoulder, shaking him gently.

"Wake up! Wake up, Honey. I know where he is. He's alive. He's OK. He's going to be fine."

"You're having a baby?" Andrew muttered. He scrunched his pillow and settled more deeply into it. "*Again?*" He went back to sleep. Angela realized he had never been awake. She decided to keep her discovery until the morning.

With the daylight, Angela's assurance wilted slightly. Had the insight and the memory been true? It had seemed so clear at 1:10 in the morning. Andrew didn't remember her trying to wake him, so she left it alone. No need to tell the whole revelation to him, maybe twice, with his hearing problem. She wondered, too, if he might turn out to be a little skeptical. But she did tell him about one other memory that had come to her in the night. She had suddenly recalled the name Dusty carried in his boyhood.

Andrew submitted to her insistence. She had more certain information to offer the authorities. He even agreed to run down to the store for her. For doughnuts. They called the Marshal's office.

On the phone Deputy Dusty's reaction was much the same as Andrew's had been in the night time.

"*Again?"* He grumbled. "You want me to come out *again?* A few days ago you claimed you knew who this suicide is. Now you claim to know *where* he is." He gave his Deputy D. snort. "You one of them seers? You know which one of them cottonwood roots he's hung up on?"

"He's not dead! I could tell you about it over the phone, but it's pretty complicated."

"I'll be there," he said.

This time Angela was prepared. The three of them hunched companionably over Andrew's doughnuts at the dining table. Zelie again waited solemnly nearby in her cone, this time in hopes of doughnut crumbs. Again the deputy glanced at her but politely made no comment.

Angela could not bear it. "That's what the javelinas did." She was about to describe the injuries and the prognosis, the need for the huge plastic protector, but she became aware of the significant silence from Andrew. The doughnuts were not too fresh. Andrew, chewing slowly and making an occasional grimace, finally spoke through his first mouthful.

"You'd better make this good," he said to Angela. He nodded at the deputy. "He's expecting it."

"Oh, yes. It's good." She beamed at Dusty. "It's good to see you again, Bernard."

Andrew choked.

"Don't mind him. He's Flemish." She laughed. Dusty didn't get it, and neither did Andrew for a short moment. Then Andrew laughed, around the remains of the doughnut. He coughed discreetly into his napkin.

"Phlegm," he said. "Get serious," he told Angela. He gave her a warning look, but she was off and running.

"Here's my idea, Bernard." She aimed another smile at him, waiting for a response.

"Idea?" the deputy said. "I thought you said you *knew.*"

"Well, I do, Bernard. I'm sure I'm right, but it's going to take a minute to explain it. Would you like another doughnut?"

Zelie wagged.

"No. Thank you." Dusty was blushing. He appeared to be occupied with something on the sleeve of his crisp uniform. He brushed it several times with the backs of his fingers.

"Oh," Angela said. "I'm sorry about that. Here..." She reached up and flicked his shirtsleeve a couple of times with her own fingers. "I keep meaning to cut those hollyhocks back. But I do like them leaning over the path. They're so friendly. You must have brushed against them. They drop a lot of pollen."

"Ain't nobody called me Bernard for a long time," he finally said, still focusing on his sleeve. "I was Bernie for a while, but when I joined the rodeo club in high school, I just took on Dusty for a name. Seemed better for a rodeo boy."

"Are you still rodeoing?" Andrew asked, raising an eyebrow at Angela and attempting to lift Dusty over the 'Bernard' speed bump.

"Nah. Ain't got time."

"But your mother called you Bernard," Angela persisted. "I remember you when you were a little boy. You went to the catechism classes with my children for a while. They were a little older than you, but I'm sure you remember them. And your mother helped with the classes. She was a very lovely person." Her instinct was to try and touch a memory in him, to bring him a bit of light. Andrew was frowning at her. "She made the best lemon poppy-seed muffins."

"Elsie Marie," Dusty acknowledged simply.

"I think my wife really might have something significant to tell you," Andrew prompted.

"Oh, yes! Yes, I do. You're going to like this, Bernard. I really think the Pilgrim is safe and I'm sure I know where he went." She saw a question and a bit of consternation leap into the deputy's eyes at this new word. Pilgrim. She had a way of complicating things. His pen had been lying idle on the clipboard, but now he took it up, preparing to write something, but not sure what it should be. "That's what I call him," she explained. "Pilgrim, because I don't know his name. Could you tell me, please?"

"Patrick. Patrick something. It's a hard one to say." He started to fumble with his clipboard, flipping the sheets backwards.

"Don't bother with that now. Patrick is good enough. Patrick is perfect, because St. Patrick's is where he went. He went to New Mexico. To a monastery. San Patricio. It's the best place in the world for him."

"How do you know that?" Andrew demanded, beating the deputy to the draw. "Does he need something from them?"

"Yeah," Dusty echoed. "How do you know that? Why'd he go there?"

"He kept something that belonged to me. A card. A holy card." She nodded happily at Andrew, then turned to the deputy. "Remember holy cards, Bernard? I bet you had some of them. He ran after my cards when they blew away, and he gave them all back to me, except for one. He wouldn't have kept it unless it meant something to him. He gave me all the others very carefully. But he was holding one of them as he sat in his car. I saw him looking at it, but at the time I didn't know what it was. And last night, in the middle of the night, I saw it again, and now I know what happened to my card." She had said all of this in a rush, but now she slowed and gave Andrew another look. "I'm so glad." She smiled at him again. "So glad, Honey."

But Deputy Dusty was unconvinced. "So what? A picture card! That ain't going to tell you where he is!"

"Of course it is! The address was on the card. He went there. To San Patricio."

"Why?" He looked from her to Andrew, incredulously. "You're telling me that some guy is going to leave a brand new Stingray and walk to New Mexico?"

"Why not?" Andrew said laconically, although Angela could see that even he was not totally convinced. Andrew tended to stick up for her most of the time. But this was a bit of a stretch.

"Why not?" Dusty repeated disgustedly to Andrew. "I can see you're married to her. You two think a lot alike."

"Why not?" Andrew said again, but he was smiling kindly at Dusty, and he flashed a grin at Angela.

"Well, I'll tell you why not." Dusty was almost shouting. "No one in his right mind would do something like that."

"No one in his right mind would commit suicide," Andrew said quietly.

"That *is* suicide! That's a funny way to kill yourself, but it's the same thing; to leave a car like that and go off to some strange place like that."

"No, Bernard," Angela said. "He was sad. A little depressed. You were right to ask about that." She stopped and thought back. "What I remember most is that he seemed confused. About himself." She realized this was true. It was exactly what she had sensed in the Pilgrim. An uncertainty. "He was trying to figure something out about his life. But he didn't want to kill himself. He wanted to help himself. He wanted to be free and clean and new."

The deputy laughed. "He's going to be real clean when we find him, that's for sure."

Angela ignored this. "He can start over at San Patricio. He can stay there as long as he wants. Forever, even."

"Forever! You said it! It could be that's where he'll stay. In the good old Verde River. Forever! He has a hundred and seventy-five miles to drift before he hits the lake. It's going to be bad news for the people who's looking for him." He glared at them. "And they're coming out. Relatives of his. Sisters. Two of them. They want to find out about him, and to pick up the Vette. And here's something else: they're not just sisters, but they're sister sisters, if you get my meaning."

"No." Andrew said. He had been listening intently to the exchange between the deputy and his wife. She could tell there were some elements in the story that were beginning to puzzle him.

"Wait." Angela pounced on Dusty. "Sisters. Do you mean…nuns?"

"Yeah. I think so. I never actually met one of them before. We don't have them in this town."

"A sinister sub-culture," Andrew said.

"Yeah. Kind of like a cult. Nothing but trouble."

"Oh, Bernard," Angela protested. "How could you say that? Where do you get such an idea? Your mom was one of the ones who wished the sisters would come here. She told me once that she had thought of becoming a nun."

"If that's true, it was a long, long time ago. She never told me about it."

"She must have told you a lot of things, Bernard. Beautiful things. I know her."

"You knew her."

"Yes."

"Now, Elsie Marie," Dusty said, apparently feeling the need to explain, "she was a good woman. You're right about that. And she did tell me lots of things. She talked about God a lot. But my dad told me that was woman's stuff. A little bit of it was good, but not to take it too far, and so I didn't."

Andrew could do nothing but sit in silence. Angela joined him in it, for the time being not having a ready response.

"Now," said the deputy, wrapping it up. "These nuns may want to talk with you when they get here. They have lots of questions. I told them their brother hasn't…surfaced…yet." He laughed quietly at his pun. When they didn't laugh with him, he added "From the river." He looked at Angela. "But you do seem to have ideas, even if they're strange ones, and you *was* the last person to actually talk with him. So maybe they'd like to hear what you have to say."

18

THEY HEARD NO MORE FROM HIM FOR A FEW DAYS, and then in the middle of an afternoon, Deputy Vada telephoned. "Those nuns are here, at last. I was right. They do want to talk with you."

Angela waited for some seconds. She was about to tell Dusty that she would be glad to speak with them, but he gave a long and eloquent sigh.

"And you was right. You was right." He said it almost regretfully. "He's alive. He's right where you said he would be. He wrote us from there. From that place in New Mexico. Says he wants to pay us for our time and trouble. DPS, too. He'll pay them, too. The guy must be rich! And crazy! But these sisters of his...I don't know if they both are really his sisters, or not. Probably just the little one is. The big one don't say much. But, like I said, they do want to talk with you about him. I told them you people was the same kind. As them."

"You, too, Bernard. You were baptized. They're the same as you."

"Sure."

And they came. Angela was watching for them the next day as they walked through the front gate. The little troupe of three stepped along in single file smartly and purposefully. Except for Deputy Dusty Vada. He seemed to be straggling behind a bit, as if distancing himself from the flavor of the group. There were indeed two sisters, a small one in front, and a taller, older, more stately one behind her.

Which would be the Pilgrim's sister sister? They were both, in their costume at least, and from a distance, beautiful. Angela's heart lifted as she saw them crossing her own yard, and she realized that, whatever their intention might be, they were bound to be a blessing for her and for Andrew.

Andrew had forbidden an exuberant greeting at the gate, and she had remembered to sequester the over-friendly and outlandishly outfitted Zelie in a bedroom. There were to be no doughnuts, only tea...and some fancy cookies whose creation had cost Angela a lot of valuable horse time. She stood at the kitchen window as they passed along the uneven pathway among her hollyhocks. Andrew came up behind her and she noticed that he was wearing his new shirt and, uncharacteristically, his hearing aids. He looked over her shoulder, studying the procession.

"Wow!" he said.

Their habits were a peachy, pale shade of pink, subdued but somehow glowing. Their veils lifted on their shoulders with their footsteps in a shimmer of the clearest blue. Angela was reminded of the sunrise she had seen that very morning. She had imagined the Virgin's colors in it, again, as she always did. Ethereal, promising, but very transitory. These Arizona sunrises always left her with a formless yearning. If she ever ran in to collect Andrew and demand that he come and see, by the time they were back outside together, the morning spectacle would have changed already, becoming a shadow of its former glory. "Yes," Andrew would agree. "How beautiful." But though he tried to see with her eyes, he would not be looking at what she had seen when she ran to fetch him.

She had a term for these poignant moments that consumed her often, the times when a beauty was almost painfully overwhelming. A beauty so grand and sacred that it cried out to be shared, or at least expressed, or kept somehow, somewhere, more profoundly. But she stood in such passing moments aching and alone, watching them slip away. To herself she called it "the loneliness of beauty," and she had never found another person who understood what she meant by it.

She had learned at last to give these moments away, offer them to God and hope that He might save them for her in eternity.

The glory of these nuns, however, was both immediate and changeless. Angela held her breath as she watched them through the window in the minutes before Andrew would go to the door and they would enter her little house. Suddenly, she experienced, like a blow, a moment of despair. Would she soon discover they were simply human, that they had ordinary human concerns? Would they diminish themselves somehow as they spoke with her? They might even, heaven forbid, be as ungrammatical as Deputy Dusty. But as they approached she allowed herself again to be enthralled by how they looked and what they stood for. They were good. This bent world did, and did not, contain them. Their wings were too bright.

"May their feet bless my land," she prayed. She knew it had already come to pass.

Inside, there were some awkward introductions. Deputy Dusty did what he could. It wasn't good.

"Oh, sisters." Angela did not have their names. Dusty had been rather mumbly about it and, truth to tell, Angela herself had thought the names were strangely similar and so had not secured them. Nor had she caught the name of their religious order, for Dusty had not given it. She had once seen something similar to their habits in a magazine article. She had forgotten the name of the order, but the habits of those nuns, who were called affectionately, "pink sisters," had been a lovely rose color. However, Angela remembered also a long swath of white scapular in the front of those habits. The garments of these sisters before her were a billow of sunny peachy pink. No white. The pale blue of the veils was an almost startling contrast. Angela wondered, though, if perhaps these sisters were of the same congregation, but in a different stage of formation. She ventured a guess. "Oh sisters," she said again. "Could you be, are you…Pink Sisters?"

"What do you think?" Dusty snorted. "You don't get any pinker than this!"

"No, we are not from the 'Pink Sisters,'" the older nun began.

"But we *are* kind of pink," said the little one.

"You are thinking of the Holy Spirit Adoration Sisters," the older one said, ignoring the interruption.

"Maybe a little salmon pink?" from Andrew.

"No," Angela said. "Sunrise pink."

The stately one gave her an appraising look. "Good thought," she said.

"Sunrise," the little one said. "And the Holy Spirit. It's His color. We do rely on the Holy Spirit." She glanced at the other woman. "Although that's not in our name."

"You must be Arizona nuns," said Angela. Why had she said this? Was it because of the Arizona-colored sunrise that had held her this morning?

"No," said the taller nun. "We are actually from Utah."

"But we *should* be Arizona nuns," said the little one. "We wear exactly the same colors as the sky was wearing here this morning as the sun came up." She did not glance again at her companion as she continued. "Maybe we *will* be Arizona nuns one day. We are a new community. And we're growing."

Angela's heart was swelling with joy. She suddenly remembered the name of the smaller nun. Mary Patricia. She and Sister Mary Patricia had watched and reveled in the same sunrise this very morning. She had not been alone with that beauty, after all. She became speechless and, to her own surprise, she remained so.

After a longish silence, Andrew rose to the occasion. Deferential, solicitous, even to the deputy, he moved among them, offering a hand to shake, looking for a purse to deposit on a chair. There were no purses. Angela wilted when she saw him bypass the living room which she had tidied, buffed and vacuumed. He directed everyone in to the dining room table, which in recent times appeared to have become the official conference center. But they looked good there, Angela thought, everyone in uniform, so to speak, and ready for business. Dusty put his clipboard on the table, and Angela brought the tea pot, cups, and plate of cookies. The cookies suddenly looked ordinary to Angela. Just butter and flour and sugar and the good toasted Camp Verde pecans. Everyone made them here. Camp Verde was beginning to be the pecan capital of Arizona. Inconsequential cookies, after all. And the powdered sugar on the outside may have been a mistake. Messy. Dusty took one gingerly between a thumb and forefinger.

"Now," he said pointedly to Angela, "suppose you tell these…ladies some of what you done told me. They know where they can find their brother. That's sure." He looked uncertainly around at this point, as if he were hoping to discover the real sister. "But they want to talk to someone who actually did speak with him before he ran…disappeared." He cleared his throat. "Of course, he's appeared again, more or less, but they want to know what he was thinking." At this point he turned and looked significantly at Andrew. "And so do I."

Andrew did not pick up on the cue. He was pouring tea for one of the sisters.

Angela began slowly. The deputy had not seemed to be sure which of the two nuns was the Pilgrim's sister. And although she had a bit of an idea, she herself was not positive. Therefore she addressed them both, smiling in encouragement. "You must be happy for your brother now. I think he's decided to do something wonderful for himself." She was not sure how much she should reveal about Pilgrim. How much did his sister know? The things he had told her in the canyon seemed to have been meant for her alone. She had not even told Andrew some of it.

"Happy." The solemn older nun gave one of her rare slow smiles. "Yes. There will be cause for rejoicing if we discover that he is truly well and has found a measure of peace. We need to determine this, for his sake and for his sister's sake." She nodded at Sister Mary Patricia.

So, as Angela had guessed, it was Sister Mary Patricia who was Pilgrim's sister. She studied the nuns quickly and discreetly. The older one was obviously in charge, definitely reserved, but helpful. She must have come as an official companion for Sister Mary Patricia. As her superior?

"My mother called us twins, but we weren't really twins," the young one said suddenly. "We just looked alike. Patrick is older. Patrick and Patricia. Can you believe my mother would do that?" She raised her eyes to Angela's, and Angela recognized the same brown deerlike luminosity that she had seen shining from the Pilgrim's.

"Twins, but not quite," Angela told her. "I see that. You almost could be. You do resemble each other. Were you close?"

"Oh, yes. Our mother named us, but our grandmother raised us." The young woman was uncertain as to how much she should say. She did not quite glance at the older nun this time. "After a while all we had was each other. Our father..." She caught herself and folded her hands in her lap.

"Patrick and Patricia. No wonder he went to San Patricio's!"

"My brother is a wonderful man; really, he is. I'm so happy to know that he's safe." She paused. "Yes, happy is a good word for what *I* feel. He's safe. And maybe *he's* happy too. Finally." She looked at Angela, an appeal. "He is, isn't he?"

"I'm sure he will be," Angela promised. "I know that good things happen at San Patricio. We'll pray for that."

Sister Mary Patricia nodded silently and darted a grateful look at her. Angela could see an extra glistening in the brown eyes.

"Wipe your nose," the older nun said to her firmly, but not unkindly.

The young one fumbled awkwardly in folds of voluminous peach, searching, apparently in vain, for a handkerchief.

Angela reached up a finger and brushed the tip of the girl's nose. "Here," she said. "Pollen. You must have been smelling my hollyhocks." She held up the pale yellow dusting on her finger for them all to see.

"Yes." The girl smiled gratefully. "The hollyhocks."

Deputy Vada was staring at the three women with a mouth that would have been agape, had he not been chewing. So far he had not taken any notes. Every once in a while he glanced at Andrew for manly solidarity, but Andrew was almost agape himself. He continued his solicitous hovering over the nuns, occasionally giving Angela a silent "do go on," command in the form of an encouraging but emphatic nod.

But Angela could not go on. She found herself speechless again. She realized, reaching back, snatching at her memory of the experience in the canyon, that the Pilgrim had chosen to reveal himself to her because he had found her to be trustworthy, and somehow safe. He had come to her as to a magnet; to her, to the dog, to the horse. Something alien to his world, but wholesome. And something had gone from her to him, something not quite of her making. It had gone out in spite of her, in spite of her stammering, resentful declarations. It had sprung partly from her natural good will toward him also, but it was not totally of herself. What was it made of, this concern for him, this softening of her heart? It was as if a fist had reached inside her and pulled out a chunk of soul.

And that fluid, refreshing, pervading light arising and descending at the end of their trail together. Could she tell all these people, even Andrew, that they had been visited by the Holy Spirit? That she might have been a channel, an instrument? Hardly. Did she believe it herself? It would take time to sort this all out. Why, when one thought about oneself, did supernatural intervention seem to be an impossibility? She believed in miracles for other people.

19

SHE HAD BATTERED HERSELF IN HER OWN MIND over all this. Looking back at the canyon encounter, she had felt no sense of triumph. His soul, his very being, may or may not have been in a state of endangerment. She didn't know everything about him. She didn't know the patterns of his life or the decisions he had made. On the other hand, in opposition to *her* opposition to his conclusions, there remained only the fact that nobody else cared. Nobody cared, one way or the other. Unless it was to supply an enthusiastic, deadly approval. She looked at the nuns. It was a relief now to know there were others who wanted something infinitely better for him.

And that light. It had been as much for her as it had been for him. Yet though the memory remained with her, it had left no lasting directive, just a continual alertness somewhere in her soul. For the Pilgrim, it must have been different. She reminded herself she had not imagined the amazed recognition she had seen in his eyes. A look that spoke of an encounter with himself.

How could she say all this? She was no mountaintop prophetess, not even a valley prophetess. From making her bold and impertinent pronouncements in the canyon, from being a hard-talking harridan, she had returned home to become once again a mealy-mouthed cookie baker. She had nothing to say.

She looked up silently, hopelessly. Andrew gazed at her, amazed, willing her to go on, but she lifted both hands in a gesture of impotence and simply said, "Yes, I spent some time with Patrick. I'm afraid I did most of the talking." She paused for another long moment, thinking, while they waited. She could not remember a thing she had told Pilgrim. As for what he had said, she could mostly remember the silences. But they were all looking at her expectantly. She had to say something. "And we walked together for a while. He did tell me some things. But mostly we had a big fight with a javelina. He was very brave. He saved my dog. I wish I could have been more helpful to him. I was not wise. I wish I had been wise."

"You had *sapientia cordis,*" Sister Mary Patricia said. "I know you did, and I'm so grateful to you. It was just what he needed. I've talked with him. He's told me so. "*Sapentia cordis.* Of course, he didn't use those words."

Angela, Andrew and Dusty gazed at the little nun. They were all in the same boat, and it was an empty one. Angela remembered only a smattering of Latin from her youth. Andrew knew some Spanish, and Deputy Dusty had an impressive command of hillbilly, but nobody knew what it was that Sister Mary Patricia had just said.

"Wisdom of the heart," the other nun explained. "She's working on her Latin. Or she's supposed to be." She looked sideways at Sister Mary Patricia. "The wisdom of the heart. It has nothing to do with the intellect."

"Then I got it," Dusty shouted. They all looked at him.

Andrew nodded in agreement. "No intellect."

But Dusty didn't notice. He had a story to tell. "I stopped an old drunk the other night, and he pulled a gun on me. My heart leaped right into my chest, as they say."

"Wasn't it already there?" Andrew asked.

"And everything to do with the Holy Spirit," the stately nun persisted, addressing Angela. "*Sapientia cordis.* Heart wisdom."

"I got the h…eck out of there," Dusty went on, "Told him to get on home. Drive safe. And all of that didn't have nothing to do with this," he tapped his head, "but everything to do with this." He thumped his chest with his fist.

"But what did that have to do with your throat?" Andrew asked.

"Huh?"

"Where your heart leaped."

"Oh, my heart just bobbled around a bunch. It didn't go nowhere."

The tall nun snatched the conversation away from the two men and spoke to Angela.

"We can discuss your encounter with Patrick at another time, dear. This nice policeman has been kind enough to lead us out here. We now have two cars in your driveway, our 'Old Reliable' and Patrick's sports car."

"I drove the Stingray," Dusty interjected dreamily.

"But we need to attend to the needs of Sister's brother in New Mexico," the older nun continued, along her practical line. "We were wondering if you would be so kind as to let us leave our older automobile behind, at your home, while we make a short visit to Patrick. We should be gone only a few days. Of course we will have to use it to drive the policeman back to his station…" Dusty gave a semi-suppressed giggle, but grew solemn as Andrew glared at him. "And then, if you could also be so kind," she looked directly at Andrew, "and if we could leave the red car here overnight, Sister Mary Patricia and I will need to learn how to manage it for the trip to New Mexico."

"To *drive* it?" Dusty asked, aghast.

"Of course. It was a gift from Patrick to his sister. We'll drive it to New Mexico, and we have need of it in our missionary work in Utah. But we will have to learn how to shift the gears." She paused and added vaguely, "And possibly there are other things."

"Well, I might…" Dusty began, but Andrew interrupted.

"Of course. I'd be glad to teach you." Andrew was too old and mellow to cast a triumphant look at Dusty, but Angela, knowing the slant of his eyes for many years, saw the sideways look, not quite triumphant, and the deputy caught it, too.

Sister Mary Patricia was beaming. She cast a grateful glance at her companion.

"Yes," she said brightly. "We can keep Patrick's car for him. We'll need both those cars in our work. We do quite a bit of traveling. We're *viators* after all."

Again Andrew, Angela and Dusty exchanged blank looks. This small nun had a way of destroying their disparity, drawing them together into a baffled brotherhood.

"Travelers," The other nun elucidated. "Sojourners. On the way."

"Pilgrims?" offered Angela.

"On the way to *Heaven.*" The older nun emphasized the word.

"That's why I said *viators.*" Sister Mary Patricia laughed. "We're headed for Heaven, but I'm sure New Mexico is nice, too."

"I had no idea you were making such progress with your Latin," her superior said. "This *is* good news!" She rolled her eyes slyly at the rest of them and smiled. "Now we'll need a plan. There's a Mass tomorrow morning at nine. Sister and I have rented a little room. We don't intend to cause you any inconvenience." She addressed this last remark to Angela. She seemed to assume, however, that Andrew's morning was fair game. "We can be here tomorrow for our driving lessons," she told him, "at about ten. We'll take the policeman back now in Old Reliable."

She rose majestically and drew the whole assembly up after her. Suddenly Angela remembered the name she had heard the deputy mumble. Another Mary it had been. Sister Mary Celeste. She also recovered the image she had been seeking, something from the arsenal of literary memories that seemed to assault her at odd hours of the day and night. Once again, it was a strong description from a Hopkins poem. A valiant nun stood among the wreckage washing across the deck of a dying ship. Sailors and passengers cowered at the masts and clung high in the rigging, but one by one they fell to the deck or were swept into the foaming sea. The nun, the leader of a small group of sisters exiled from Germany, remained standing tall upon the deck, in the gale of flying snow and lashing waves. "A lioness," Hopkins called her, a "prophetess" towering in the tumult.

She had called encouragement to the men in the rigging, and powerfully beyond them, to her Christ, her savior. She had not survived, but survivors of "The Wreck of the Deutschland," an actual historical event, had reported her heroic actions for Hopkins to immortalize.

Now, here for Angela was someone of similar stature. There was something commanding, transcendent about Sister Mary Celeste, standing tall in their kitchen. They were in the presence of greatness. Angela could see that Andrew was awed, as well.

But Dusty refused to look at her, addressing himself instead to the younger nun. He cleared his throat thoughtfully and gave his chin a rub. Politely, he began to inquire. "You're kind of a cute little gal," he assured her. "What made you want to do this?" He made a restrained gesture at her garments.

There was a flash of startled brown eyes. Then a silence.

"She'll tell you all about it on her way out to the car." Sister Mary Celeste gave an emphatic nod to Sister Mary Patricia, and Angela caught the quick wink behind Dusty's back.

The little entourage left the house and trooped in single file back down the walkway after Sister Mary Celeste. Angela wondered why she and Andrew should feel compelled to follow, but they did. She noticed that Sister Mary Patricia smiled at the hollyhocks, but refrained from sniffing them. Obediently the little nun began the conversation with the deputy, speaking back at him over her shoulder.

She began haltingly. "I'm very happy with…this." Angela could hear her voice become steady and begin to lilt, as she explained her way of life to him.

Dusty listened attentively.

"There's a whole other world," Sister Mary Patricia concluded. "An invisible world. It's more real than this one. More alive, and it goes on forever. But it's connected with this one. So we really are already living in two worlds. But in this one, in this world," she struggled for a minute with her idea. "We who are consecrated, we who are religious, we are expressions of God."

"Expressions of God," the deputy repeated.

Sister Mary Celeste halted suddenly at the sound of LB's whinny. Sister Mary Patricia stopped abruptly behind her, and Dusty, following, stumbled up against the hem of her habit. He sprang back as if he'd been stung.

"Oh," Sister Mary Celeste breathed. "An Arab!" She stood for a moment.

They followed her gaze. Over the corral fence Little Big Man stared at them, wide-eyed and alert. His black forelock had been blown to the side. He seemed to be deliberately displaying the white star on his beautiful forehead.

Suddenly Sister Mary Celeste was running, floating, over the lawn to the corral. The sunrise habit billowed behind her, and Angela wondered, stupidly, what sort of shoes she must be wearing. She found herself hoping they were not black and clunky, but she couldn't see. The rest of them remained in line, watching. Sister Mary Patricia stood rapt in amazement for a moment. She made a move to follow her superior, but then apparently thought better of it.

LB did not startle at the majestic creature flying toward him. The celestial creature, Angela thought. He stood his ground, waiting. When she reached the horse, the nun held his face between her hands, gazing into his eyes for a long moment. Then she put her own face against his nose. He did not move.

Angela and Andrew exchanged glances. Sister Mary Patricia turned to them with a look of wonder. Deputy Vada glanced surreptitiously at his watch.

And then Sister Mary Celeste was walking swiftly toward them again. She made no word of explanation, but continued the parade to the gate. Dusty darted around her to open it for them all, and she swept through, giving him a nod.

The Pilgrim's red sports car made a statement in their driveway. The other car, "Old Reliable," made its own statement. It, too, was long and low, possibly longer than the Corvette. It was indeed a long, long car. Inelegant now, it seemed to make a claim to former grandeur. It had once been a rich, gold color, which still showed through in the protected places, but most of it had faded to tan and anemic yellow. Apparently the roof had been covered with something that resembled a brocaded fabric. This was shredded and water stained. One longish piece trailed over the back window. Angela could picture it when the car was in motion as a festive pennant flying behind them. But apparently it was a new development, and problematic, for Sister Mary Celeste frowned at the car slightly, then reached up and tore it off. She handed the fragment to Angela.

The old sedan had four wide doors. Dusty looked wistfully at the Stingray, then opened the back door of the older car, made a grimace, and settled himself inside. Andrew opened a front door for Sister Mary Patricia, and then moved to the driver's side for Sister Mary Celeste. But she paused for a moment, and looked steadily at them.

"I loved horses once," she said. She smiled at herself, as if in recognition of an abandoned but still viable truth. "I guess I still do."

She got into the car and wheeled its bulk expertly around. Angela saw Dusty's hand rise from the obscurity of the backseat to steady himself against the window. The driver had rolled her own window down.

"We'll be here tomorrow for our driving lessons," she called to Andrew. "Will we see you at Mass before then?"

"Yes, of course," he said. Angela glanced at him in surprise. Tomorrow was Wednesday and he had an appointment for his own truck at the garage. "This is important," he had told Angela. "I have to be there early, and you need to follow me down and drive me back. Don't let us forget."

He caught her gaze now and shrugged.

20

THE SUNRISE SISTERS HAD CAUSED A BIT OF A STIR at the local parish when they appeared at the midweek Mass. Though they had been surrounded by appreciative well-wishers afterwards, they had managed to escape and to appear on time for their appointment with Andrew. He was ready.

Angela had planned a breakfast for them all, but Sister Mary Celeste was eager to get on with the business at hand. Angela went out with them to stand among the assortment of cars, trucks, trailers and one old Jeep, which made an impressive collection in their driveway. Andrew laid out his plan. As he talked, she went over to look in the Stingray's window. The leather steering wheel looked leathery indeed, and comfortable, but the leather seats did not look too promising. Like little nests, they huddled low on the floor below an instrument panel of imposing complexity. Andrew was to sit in here, apparently, with his knees drawn up, and entrust his life to someone enveloped in a blanket's worth of fabric, who would be gripping that leather wheel with two small hands, and plunging invisible cloth-draped feet among a selection of pedals, while ramming a stubby stick shift in various directions.

Andrew explained the rudiments of sports car driving and then settled himself in behind the wheel for a moment to check out the array of switches and buttons. Angela, embarrassed by her ignorance of automobile lore, decided to check out Old Reliable. What a difference between the two vehicles that were approximately the same dimension. Old Reliable had seen a lot of road time. A faded bumper sticker still partially adhering to the chrome advised: "Get your kicks on Route 66." Angela doubted the sisters had attached that sticker. She wondered about the old veteran's history. The insignia named it a Chrysler Cordova. Angela had asked Andrew about the roof covering. A landau top, he told her. For what it was worth. Compared to the Stingray, the interior of the car was vast. There were arm rests on all four of the wide doors, and silvery handles with knobs to roll down the windows. One of the knobs was missing, and someone had covered the stump with duct tape. A substantial shelf under the back window contained nothing but a box of Kleenex. Apparently the massive trunk area contained everything the sisters might need. The back seat was wide enough for a good nap. There was something hospitable about the ancient car, but Angela wondered how much stamina remained in it. No wonder the sisters were driving the sports car to New Mexico. Old Reliable looked weary.

Sister Mary Patricia was to go first. Andrew crawled out of the driver's seat to trade places with her. He had a glazed look about his eyes, and when neither of the sisters was looking, he flashed Angela an eye roll, a shrug, and a what-have-I gotten-myself-into look, with a gesture back at the car. She had no answer for him.

"It's a little bit complicated in there," he said. "I'd better take her for a short spin around the block first. As it were." He maneuvered himself back in and Sister Mary Patricia folded herself and all her clothing into the low seat beside him.

The blocks in their neighborhood were acres across. Angela wondered if the engine needed to roar quite as much as Andrew seemed to be demanding of it. He lurched a little backing up, and lurched again a few times as he drove away. From a distance she heard him roaring at the stop sign. After ten minutes or so, he could be heard roaring back slowly from the opposite direction, but by the time they drove up the driveway, he had gentled the car down to a subdued purr.

"I've got the hang of this thing," he announced. "I think." He sat there for a while, grinning. Now it was Sister Mary Patricia's turn. They traded places. It took some time.

Angela invited Sister Mary Celeste inside for coffee, but she declined, holding up her breviary. "I think I might need to pray." To Angela's surprise, the dignified woman gave *her* a wink. "I'll wait in here." She pointed at the old car. "But for now I need to keep watching and listening to my instructor." She leaned down attentively to the open windows of the Stingray, where Sister Mary Patricia and Andrew huddled, discussing the merits of their red rocket.

Angela could bear it no longer. She went inside to reassemble the breakfast and turn it into brunch.

She hummed as she worked, trying not to listen, but among the roaring and the sudden commanding silences, she thought she discerned at one or two points something that sounded like a metallic scraping. Once, yes, decidedly, she heard a solid crunch. But it could have been a neighbor dropping a hay bale from his barn loft into his pickup bed. And no one came running in, bleeding.

"Give us an hour," Andrew had said. "This big old tank they've been driving has an automatic transmission, one of the earlier ones. The Stingray will be quite a change."

In an hour and a half they came trooping in. Angela examined them. They were all looking slightly bedraggled and ready for refreshment. Andrew, in fact, was looking much the worse for wear.

"Well," he announced, "quite an escapade. Daunting. Kind of a disaster, actually. Probably not any worse than your dog's ear, though. Let's just say we have another badge of honor."

"What badge? My new truck?"

"No. My truck. And it was just the trailer hitch. It's tough, so it's just a little bit askew. We hardly ever use that truck with the trailer, anyway." He smiled at the sisters. "But Dusty is probably not going to be too happy."

"What does he care about your trailer hitch?"

"It's what it did to the Stingray."

"Oh."

"A little hole in the fender. Ain't gonna slow 'er down none, though," he said in Dusty tones. He cleared his throat carefully and then added, "Two badges of honor, actually."

"Two! What else?"

"Well, a scrape on another Stingray fender that came from the horse trailer."

"My horse trailer?"

"That's the only one we have."

"That scrape was mine," said Sister Mary Celeste humbly. "I suppose you would have to say two scrapes: on the car and on the horse trailer."

"That makes four badges of honor, altogether." Angela tried to say it lightly.

"At the very least," Andrew said, without looking at her.

She popped her eyes at the OA, but he refused to elaborate. He picked up one of her scones and examined it appreciatively.

Zelie, given a conditional invitation to the dining area, was on her best behavior. She sat at attention without her plastic ruff at last, the classic black and tan hound, her ears drooping, her eyes alert, her body lean and muscular, and her tail tapping gently against one of the cabinets. The sisters exclaimed over her beauty and her manners.

"*Qui me amat, amet canum meam,*"said Sister Mary Patricia, smiling at Angela.

"Oh, I know that one!" Angela exclaimed. "Who loves me, loves my dog. I do know some Latin! I wish I could remember how to say that."

"Stick with her," Sister Mary Celeste said dryly. "She'll teach you everything of liturgical significance that you'll ever need to know."

So far Sister Mary Patricia had not taken a bite of anything. She sat silently for a moment, gazing beyond them all. Then she spoke in a voice full of awe. "I've never done anything like that. First we leaped forward. Then we leaped backward. Then in between those leaps the engine stalled. What do they expect you to do with all those pedals and only two feet? And hundreds of directions for the gear shift to go in. No wonder Patrick left that car behind." She sat for a minute, reminiscing. "But, you know, once I really got going it was pretty nice. There *is* something about all that power. Just waiting to be turned loose. It will be fun," she gave a little gulp and glanced at her superior with widened eyes; but she pushed on, "to use every one of those gears. To see what she will do on the open road."

"She?" said Sister Mary Celeste. "You feel the same sense of restrained but potential power on a well-trained horse." She paused. "And, I might add, the same sense of out-of-control power, if you don't know what you're doing."

"I think she'll manage pretty well," Andrew said, nodding at Sister Mary Patricia. "Now you, on the other hand," he said to Sister Mary Celeste, "could use a little more practice."

The older nun dropped her eyes humbly. "Sister Mary Patricia will do the driving. When we come back from New Mexico, we'll take both cars to Utah with us. Then we'll decide what to do with them." She caught the silent plea in the younger woman's eyes. "Old Reliable might be just the right thing for a large and needy family. The red car would possibly be useful for a couple of nuns. In any case, she'll be put to good use."

21

THE BRUNCH OVER, the small amount of earthly possessions transferred from Cordova to Corvette, one more long practice run for Sister Mary Patricia in which she was able to try out a few more gears, and good-byes were said. Andrew made the sign of the cross over the red car as she rumbled east toward New Mexico. To Angela the car bore a whole new personality as it carried the two nuns away. A Stingray on a mission.

Angela had walked with them all to the gate and stood with Sister Mary Celeste as she waited during Sister Mary Patricia's final driving lesson. LB had called to them again from the corral as they left the yard, but the nun had not crossed over to him. She ignored him, stepping determinedly along, leading the way. Out among the various vehicles, she wandered slowly, serene and erect, her hands clasped. She seemed to be lost in thought. Pleasant to Angela, still she did not invite conversation. Once in a while she glanced upward, but not so much in appeal as in a challenge and an invitation. Angela thought again of the tall nun on the deck of the doomed ship in Hopkins' poem, standing among the masts and shifting cargo, a stern and yet comforting presence for the terrified passengers and crew. Offering them Christ, the only thing she had to give. This nun, Sister Mary Celeste, also shone with a formidable and selfless courage. Here was heroism, but not as the world understood it.

And now the nuns were gone. Angela turned to Andrew. She felt a sense of profound loss and diminishment, the way they both had felt when their children left home for their college adventures. She searched for something to say to mitigate the vacancy that she imagined in him. Something cheerful. It occurred to her suddenly that this was The Year of Consecrated Life, declared officially by the Church for that intention.

"What a gift this visit has been for us," she said to him, "in this special year. What a thing to happen to us in this year for consecrated people."

Andrew had already removed his detested hearing aids, his 'ear phones,' as he called them. "Beer and complicated pickles," he said now. "Sounds good. But those pickles aren't really complicated. Just the same old dill. They look different because I got them at the farmers' market, and that lady puts lots of exotic herbs in them. Some kind of weed."

"Dill."

"Yeah."

Angela stood mystified for a long moment. This happened sometimes. Usually, if she gave herself enough time his meaning would become clear. Or she would think back and find a way to hear what he thought *he* had heard.

"Beer," he said again. He began quietly listing things to himself. "And salami. No. Prosciutto. Cheddar, Brie, crackers and those good dilly pickles. It's a little early, but we can make an afternoon picnic out of it. I'll start working on it." He saw her staring wonderingly at him. "Why are you standing there?"

She followed him slowly into the house. What had she said to him? She had to figure it out. Sometimes she let these things go, but with the prospect of routine descending on them once again she felt she had new leisure to unravel verbal entanglements. She had been thinking about Pope Francis's dedication of this year to all the members of religious orders who did so much good around the world, brought so much light into the darkness. Bright wings, for sure. Many bright wings. Hope for the world. But that's not what she had said. Consecrated. That was it. The sisters who had visited them were consecrated. The religious brothers who maintained San Patricio's were consecrated. Maybe even Pilgrim could someday be established among them. Consecrated.

Suddenly it dawned on her. "Consecrated people!" she flung at Andrew, laughing. "You dummy!" I said 'year for consecrated people,' not 'beer and complicated pickles.'"

"I knew it all the time," he said solemnly. "Just stringing you along."

But she permitted herself the faintest of skeptical smiles. How she had loved him all these years. The last husband.

22

Deputy Dusty Vada stopped by briefly once in the nuns' absence. He came, he said, to tie up a few loose ends in the investigation, and he carried his clipboard. But he seemed to be obsessed with a weightier dilemma.

Finally he got down to it. "Just what are you people up to?" he demanded. "You take these gals away from a perfectly good life, lock them up somewhere together. They don't get to see nothing of the real world. That ain't normal."

"You'd prefer to see them remain trapped in a world where little girls are groomed to be seductive and promiscuous? Where the greatest good seems to be having and acquiring?" Andrew waited, but there was no answer. He was about to say another "where," when Dusty spoke.

"And then some guy decides to do pretty much the same thing. He walks off into the sunset, leaving a Stingray just sitting empty behind him. He falls off the face of the earth. You call any of that normal?"

"No," Andrew said, "I suppose no one would call that normal. It's pretty darned beautiful, though. Those people have chosen the better part. They want to live a life closer to God. You and I, Deputy, we have to slog along in the muck of everyday life. You have to admit it's a struggle."

"Oh, but Honey," Angela protested, "they have to struggle too. There's struggle in everyone's life."

"You ain't just whistlin' Dixie!" Dusty exploded. "Struggle is my middle name. I done saw one of the most beautiful women I ever seen in my life, and I have to pretend I never laid eyes on her!"

"Oh, Bernard," Angela whispered, suddenly enlightened. "Oh, Bernard. You're talking about little Sister Mary Patricia, aren't you?"

"Sister Mary this, Sister Mary that! How come they all have to be named Mary? They weren't born that way!"

"It's a beautiful name, Bernard. They chose it to honor the mother of God. Don't you think that's lovely? She was the most perfect human being who ever lived."

"Nobody's perfect. It ain't natural."

"Mary was. She was perfect *and* natural. And she was very brave."

"Now I did know one brave woman in my life," Dusty said. "And I don't mean you. What you do is just plain stupid, going off by yourself all the time like that."

And here was Andrew, doing his javelina bristle again. She could almost hear his teeth grinding, javelina style. Once again Angela found herself smashing the toe of his boot with her foot. She thought quickly.

"Your mother," she guessed. "You're thinking about Elsie. Yes, she was brave."

"Elsie Marie. Now there was a woman." He sat quietly, remembering.

"And guess what, Bernard? She was *another* Mary."

"No!" But he looked at her questioningly.

"Marie is a way of saying Mary."

"Well, I'll be…Mary after Mary after Mary." But he was pleased, she could tell.

"Your father must be missing her terribly," Andrew said.

"Jack? Nah, he's got himself a girlfriend."

"The old fool." Andrew shook his head.

"Yeah." The deputy rose with his clipboard untouched. But it seemed he still had something on his mind. "Now this is what I don't get. That guy has called me a couple of times. More than a couple of times. That brother. First he wanted to talk about the money he owed. Then, of course, he wanted to see about those two sisters. Then he wanted to see if I knew you people. Meaning you." He peered at Angela. "Now he's talking the way you talk, the way you all talk. It don't make sense. First he was missing. Then he wasn't missing. I'm beginning to wish he was missing again. Somehow he found out I used to be, you know, the way you all still are. He's trying to tell me how good it is for him there. Where he is. How he's changing. He's starting to sound like my mother. On and on. I try to tell him something, he calls me on it. He's got all the answers. And I mean *all* the answers. Got every answer known to man."

"But that's just it, Bernard," Angela protested. "If something's worth anything, then it's worth telling somebody about. He's telling you about something important."

The deputy pushed his chair under the table and turned to go. "I still can't see nothing but a waste," he muttered, shaking his head. "Waste of a good car. Waste of a really good little gal." He stood for a moment, pondering. "Maybe I need to talk with those gals for a minute again when they come back through here."

"No, Bernard."

He left, and for some time they heard nothing more from him.

And then the sisters were back from New Mexico. 'The gals,' as Andrew was beginning to call them, but only to Angela.

They arrived in town without any Dusty fanfare, made a polite and informative visit to Andrew and Angela, gathered the keys for Old Reliable, and were on their way back to Utah. They promised to hold each other in prayer and to otherwise keep in contact. Andrew assured them that he and Angela would visit them in the near future. Angela skewed her eyes around at him as he said this. The OA leaving town? She nodded and smiled agreeably for his sake.

They had walked out with the sisters to say goodbye. There in the driveway stood Old Reliable, solid and dependable, if a trifle ugly. In the nuns' absence Andrew had taken the car out once to have the tires checked and the gas tank filled. Otherwise, it had not gone anywhere. Beside it again squatted the red rocket. The car looked as if it had been on and off the highways of New Mexico for months. It carried a great number of smeared bug carcasses and dings, and an impressive coating of New Mexico dust and mud. Mostly dust, because the great southwest had been suffering a long drought. But somewhere the car had encountered a substantial mud hole. The spoke wheels were encrusted with dried mud which had also hardened around the head and tail lights. One of the side view mirrors was truncated. Andrew reached a tender hand to what was left of it. "Badge of honor," he said.

"And another badge of honor on the other side," Sister Mary Patricia admitted honestly. "Low down on the door. But she carried us through. She doesn't get great gas mileage, but she's better than Old Reliable." She looked sideways at Sister Mary Celeste. Then she looked closely at Angela and took her hand, holding it gently for a moment. "Patrick's happy again," she said quietly. "He's almost his old self. I don't know what his plans are. But," she smiled. "He did say I could keep the car! Or *we* could keep the car."

"And we must be leaving." Sister Mary Celeste touched no one's hand. But with her clear eyes she gave Andrew and Angela, each in turn, a long look.

"Always leaving," Sister Mary Patricia added. "We're *viators*, after all."

The nuns jockeyed the vehicles around each other and left Arizona, Old Reliable leading the way, the Stingray throbbing along closely behind. It was a mismatched convoy of two, the odd couple. But in purpose, they were somehow complementary.

Again, Andrew made the sign of the cross over them, and except for the rumbling of an engine and the rattling of a loose exhaust pipe, they were soon out of hearing.

Their lives returned to normal. No more needy strangers, no javelinas, no nuns, no officers of the law. Just the two of them and their ordinary comfortable chores, their conversations on philosophy, theology and literature. The discourse with flora and fauna on their own property. Foolishness, laughter, a little worry; the wise and lovely rhythm of the liturgical year with its feasting and fasting. The easy, loving companionship of years of marriage. Everything in the context of prayer, silent or expressed in their own personal community. “God has entrusted the earth to the alliance between man and woman,” Pope Francis had said. It was good. It was enough.

23

THEY WERE IN THE MIDDLE OF THEIR MORNING PRAYERS one day when Zelie jumped to her feet, baying.

"Oh, no," Andrew moaned. "Someone's at the front gate." He put aside his breviary, went to look out a window, and made his report. "There's a couple of guys out there I don't recognize. Better go see what they want." He peered at Angela in make-believe fierceness. "What have you done now?"

She laughed.

Zelie was clamoring and dancing in excitement. He tried to keep her inside, but she burst past him as he opened the door. Angela went to a window, too, and watched the dog as she streaked toward the two men standing just inside the gate. One, a cowboy, seemed to be pointing out features of her property to the other and explaining something earnestly to him. They walked toward the house. Was the cowboy a real estate agent? A "horse property" specialist? Had Andrew secretly put their home up for sale? They had discussed that eventuality, but would Andrew have made such a decision without consulting her? Yes, he might, she had to concede. He had recently bought a large, lime-green solar-powered frog light for the garden. "Why?" she had asked. "I don't know," he had replied. What an Andrew.

He had now captured the dog, but still he seemed to be as puzzled by these visitors as Angela was. He stood uncertainly on the pathway, hunched over, grasping Zelie's collar, focused on the two men. There was a brief scuffle, and the hound was free. Angela recognized the moment when he realized Zelie was totally out of his control. It was identical to many of her own moments with Zelie. Andrew's shoulders sagged slightly in resignation.

The cowboy walked in front. The hound hurtled past him and accosted the second man with exuberant joy. There was something about him. Angela could not see his face well, but there was something familiar about his military posture and his gait.

Andrew now appeared to recognize someone. He moved forward, extending his hand. Then he stood back to look appraisingly at the cowboy and make a statement about his appearance. Angela recognized him too, suddenly. Dusty! He was out of uniform, or rather, he was *in* uniform. He wore a fancy Stetson, shaped just so in front, not too much turn-down at the brim, Arizona correct. Wranglers. Understated denim shirt, and a pair of good looking alligator boots.

The other man had moved up beside him and now he stood still on the path. Zelie had risen on her hind legs and remained balanced there with her front feet clamped to his chest. He reached for her head with both hands to look into her eyes, and when she dropped back to the ground, he leaned over, picked up her almost mended ear and examined it closely. Then he held the ear in one hand and pulled the whole thing gently through his fingers.

It was the Pilgrim! Angela ran out into the yard.

"Look who I done brought," the cowboy said.

"Bernard!" At this exclamation from her, the two men exchanged glances.

"That's my other name," Dusty said.

"And a good one," the Pilgrim said. "Why didn't you tell me?"

"Why do you think?"

Angela stood gazing at the Pilgrim, suddenly self-conscious. Did he expect her, by now, to know his real name? He had never told her.

Dusty supplied. "You think *I* got a funny name. What do think this lady calls you?" He paused. "Pilgrim! She calls you Pilgrim." He waited for the reaction.

Now it was Angela and the Pilgrim who exchanged glances. Pilgrim's mouth curled slightly and his eye corners crinkled in the same way as Sister Mary Patricia's, but his manner remained solemn.

"I wanted to call you first, to give you a warning," he said. "But Bernard here, insisted that we should just come on out."

"Yeah," Dusty said. "I thought we should surprise you, you being buddies and all. Almost buddies, anyway. You was the one to keep saying, 'He ain't dead. He ain't dead.' Turns out he *ain't* dead. Turns out he's just been having an adventure. He's been telling me about it. Says he wants me to see it."

Angela examined him. "Bernard, you're ..." She tried to think of something adequate for him. "You're really a cowboy. You're just simply a true cowboy. You're...more a Dusty than a Bernard."

She seemed to have a wonderful capacity for making the deputy blush.

"I know," he said. "This is the real me." He looked down at his boots and then at Angela and added ruefully, "What a waste."

She squinched her eyes at him slightly and shook her head. "No, not a waste."

"Yeah," he said. "Maybe you're right. And there's still a little Bernard left in me. My mother would want that."

"You're really Patrick, I know," she said, turning to the Pilgrim. "And your little sister is one of the loveliest people I've ever met."

"Yes, she is. Truly. She's the light of my life." He tilted his head toward Angela and nodded. "And then there's that other. That great light."

So he did remember.

"San Patricio's," she said tentatively. "Has that been good for you?"

"Good. Yes."

"Would your grandmother be happy?"

He laughed. "They have the sacraments there. *All* the sacraments."

She hesitated, shrinking a little before Andrew's scrutiny. "Guilt?" she ventured, not catching anyone's eye.

"Guiltlessness. You don't have to live with every mistake you ever made."

Andrew had been measuring this conversation. Some elucidation was going to be due him later in the afternoon. Andrew was a pretty shrewd dude, after all. And, sooner or later, she realized, she was also going to have to tell him the story of her dangling over the off side of Little Big Man. They had always been truth to each other.

Dusty became official. "He wanted to see you," he said. "Says he has something to give you. He came out here to settle up with us. All of us. He came out here on a bus." He couldn't help rolling his eyes at Andrew. "A bus!"

"The inside of a bus is good for the outside of a man," Patrick said. He and Angela shared another glance and a smile.

"But he's not going *back* on a bus," Dusty announced.

"No, I'm going in style."

Dusty had been cogitating mightily. "What I don't get," he said slowly, "is how you got out to New Mexico in the first place. You couldn't have gone all that way on foot."

"I'll tell you all about it on our way back. It was quite an adventure. No buses that time."

"Back?" Andrew said vaguely, as if he hadn't heard properly. Maybe he hadn't.

"I got some time off coming," Dusty explained. "I'm driving him back. No more bus for him! He's going in a good old Ford pickup truck. He done got himself a *chauffeur!*" Dusty said the last word with what he considered to be a French flourish.

Andrew suddenly sharpened up. He turned and stared at Patrick in amazement. "You're going back? To New Mexico? With *him*?"

"Oh yes," Patrick said. "He wants to do this. I've been nagging him some over the phone. He's been having a hard time figuring out why I went there to begin with." Patrick seemed to regard Dusty with respect, which caused Angela, and she could see, Andrew as well, to take a new look at the deputy.

"Got to see what's there," Dusty said, "what's the big attraction."

"But you don't know him." Andrew insisted, still addressing Patrick.

"Oh, he does, he does," Dusty said. "I told you we've been talking. And he's been calling from that place, whatever it is, quite a bit. Ever since he got found." He stopped for a moment, as if he were searching his memory. "He was lost and now he's found. Seems like there was a song about that somewhere."

"Yeah," Andrew said. "Amazing Grace. You're getting pretty good, Deputy." He cleared his throat. "Are you," he cleared his throat again. "Are you prepared to stay there a while?"

Dusty's eyes widened. "Me? No! That ain't for me. I'm too old for that sort of stuff."

"He's kind of interested." Patrick said. "He'll stay long enough to get the flavor of the place. They're having a retreat." He raised his eyebrows and pursed his lips before he added quietly, "A silent retreat." Dusty was staring at him.

"What I said was…I just wanted to know…" Dusty protested.

"It's a good flavor," Patrick assured him.

"I don't want to be a waste," Dusty reminded them. He looked down again at his alligator boots. "And I ain't taking no chances." He turned to Angela. "But Elsie Marie told me to do this thing. She does talk to me sometimes." He said this matter-of-factly.

"You'll like it," Patrick promised. "They have some wise people there. They know how to give you what you need. And take away what you don't need."

"What would they take away?" Dusty asked suspiciously.

"Don't worry about the boots. You can keep the boots. You're going with the boots and you're coming back with them. And, I'm grateful for the ride."

"You'll like *that*! It's no Stingray, but it's a Ford F-250. We can put the hammer down! Haul whatever we want."

"I can't wait." Patrick caught Andrew's eyes. Then he looked at Angela. "But I came back out here because I have a debt to pay to these good people." He made a gesture at Dusty. "So many people." He continued to gaze at her. "Mostly to you, though. I owe you a debt I can't repay. But I do have something for you." He reached into a pocket and handed Angela a card, her holy card. San Patricio, the wall, the bougainvillea, the little blue gate. And on the back, the selection from the *De Profundis*. "Out of the depths I cry to you, Oh Lord. Lord, hear my prayer…" She read that entire portion of the psalm now to herself without looking up at any of them. She held the card for a moment, then handed it to Dusty.

"This is for you, Bernard."

"Oh," he said. "I don't know. You people." They all looked at him. "No way I can figure any of you out. You waste women." He suddenly had the faraway Stingray look in his eyes. "And you waste good automobiles. And now you want me to be a waste." This time it was Andrew who squinted his eyes and shook his head.

Dusty ducked his own head, then raised it again to speak to them. "I'll probably be seeing you people when I come back." Angela felt Andrew snag a breath. She smiled at Dusty, understanding his need to say another thing. He kicked gently at a tuft of grass beside the pathway. "I might just run into you two at that little church up on the hill." He added warily, "Might, I said."

But Patrick laughed. "You're good, Bernie," he said. "You're good to go." He looked at Angela and Andrew. "As for me," he said, "I may or may not stay. I'm an architect." Angela nodded. "They want me to stay a while, at least. To find a way to let more light into their old buildings. Light. Light and more light." He smiled at himself. "They're trusting *me* to bring light!"

"You know light," Angela said.

"You're one of them?" Dusty blurted. "You're wise, too? *Sapientia cordis?*" He pronounced it correctly. "Don't tell me you got it too! It's like a disease around here!"

Patrick looked startled.

"You don't know what that means!" Dusty said disgustedly. "I can explain it to you on the way. Turns out there might be some things I can teach *you*."

"I'm sure that's true," Patrick told him.

"Let's do it," Dusty said. He put the card in his pocket.

Patrick turned again to Angela and Andrew. "One thing's for sure," he told them, "wherever I go, whatever I do, or if I stay at San Patricio, I'll never be the same."

"Me neither, probably," Dusty muttered grimly.

Angela embraced each of them briefly before they turned away.

She and Andrew remained standing in the yard for a while. Zelie's cold nose found the back of her hand. She ran her fingers over the scarred and puckered ear. Little Big Man called over the fence and she went to him. The last hound, the last horse, the last husband. She was content.

CPSIA information can be obtained
at www.ICGtesting.com
Printed in the USA
FSOW01n0248211115
13597FS